For thirteen years now *Perry Rhodan* has been acknowledged to be the world's top-selling science fiction series. Originally published in magazine form in Germany, the series has now appeared in hardback and paperback in the States.

Over five hundred *Perry Rhodan* clubs exist on the Continent and *Perry Rhodan* fan conventions are held annually. The first *Perry Rhodan* film, 'S.O.S. From Outer Space', has now also been released in Europe.

The series has sold over *100 million* copies in Europe alone.

Also available in the *Perry Rhodan* series

Clark Darlton

Perry Rhodan 6

The Secret of the Time Vault

Futura Publications Limited
An Orbit Book

An Orbit Book

First published in Great Britain in 1975
by Futura Publications Limited

Copyright © Ace Publishing Corporation 1971

The series was created by Walter Ernsting and Karl-
Herbert Scheer, translated by Wendayne Ackerman and
edited by Donald A. Wollheim and Forrest J. Ackerman.

ISBN 0 8600 78426
Printed in Great Britain by
Hazell Watson & Viney Ltd
Aylesbury, Bucks

Futura Publications Limited
49 Poland Street,
London W1A 2LG

Chapter One

RHODAN 'CONQUERS' GALACTO-CITY

The gigantic spacesphere was hurtling across the orbital plane of the forty-second planet of the sun Vega. It went into the faster-than-light drive and set course for the planet Earth, twenty-seven light-years distant.

And then it happened.

The huge ship, in an instant, became invisible. It simply dissolved, dematerialized, disappeared as if it had never existed.

Such is the transition from the fourth into the fifth dimension.

But no four-dimensional body can consciously exist inside fifth-dimensional space, in which neither three-dimensional measuring scales nor chronological calibrations have any meaning. The body ceases to be matter subject to the laws of the space-time continuum. It becomes timeless.

Nevertheless, it exists!

Thus the colossal spacecraft, eight hundred yards in diameter, continued to exist, but in another form. So did its passengers.

Perry Rhodan's mind was filled with serious doubts as he issued the order for the hyperspace jump via the automatically guided electronic brain, for, after all, he was unfamiliar with the ship. It was an alien craft, captured in another solar system, wrested from the Topides, a non-human race, who in turn had seized the spacesphere from its original owners, the Arkonides – legendary rulers of the universe. Fortunately, the ship's technical design resembled that of the disabled *Good Hope*, the ship that had brought Rhodan into this sector of the universe, where he had become embroiled in a series of battles with the lizard-like Topides.

Rhodan realized the risk that lay in attempting transition to Earth with an unfamiliar and undermanned ship. However, he had no alternative, if he wanted to help the inhabitants of Ferrol, the eighth Vegan planet, in their fight to rid themselves of the invaders of their world. Unaided, the Ferrons were simply incapable of overcoming the inimicable Topides.

Such was the motivating force behind Rhodan's daring decision to risk the hyperspace jump which might well mean death and the end of all his plans for mankind and the universe entire.

There was but a single entity aboard the *Stardust II* – as Rhodan privately thought of the conquered vessel – that could consciously experience the jump through space and time: the positronic brain. It automatically stored all sensory impressions of the dematerialized crew, retaining the information for future use. Additionally, the positronic brain took care to activate the robot crew as soon as rematerialization took place, so that the robots' human charges would be guarded from any possible harm.

To Rhodan, no time seemed to have passed from the moment the spacesphere began its hyperspace jump. But a tremendous pain raged throughout his body. He felt as if he were about to be torn apart and was completely incapable of so much as moving a finger.

His friend Reginald Bell, companion of lunar adventures a few years earlier, was lying on the other side of the command center, moaning softly, eyes wide open and staring at the ceiling.

The door opened silently and a human shape entered the

8

command center, glistening metallically in the subdued light. It was one of the special robots which, having been ordered to do so by the positronic brain, now obeyed the new masters of the spaceship without hesitation. Gently it applied self-acting injection patches to its human charges.

Perry Rhodan's intense pain subsided instantly. He sat up and regarded the automatic calendar. Some time had passed, of course, but the calendar had been adjusted to Earth time. A short span – but during it they had traveled twenty-seven light-years!

Suddenly Rhodan realized that the two shipwrecked Arkonides natives, Khrest and Thora, could now return to Arkon whenever they pleased, even though their home planet was more than 32,000 light-years distant from Earth. All along they had been eager to do so, but Rhodan had so far skillfully thwarted their attempts, for Earth's exact location in the universe had to be kept a secret at all costs. Mankind was not yet ready to become a decisive factor in cosmic politics, therefore it was wiser to keep out of it until the time was ripe.

Bell sat up slowly, then swung his legs over the edge of his couch onto the floor, whose covering, like the rest of the spaceship, seemed somehow to have mysteriously withstood thousands of years of use. Bell yawned.

'I've slept an eternity, but I'm tireder than I was before. Did it work all right?'

Rhodan nodded. 'Yes, the transition has worked fine . . . so far, at least. We have to check our position first, though, then we'll know for sure. I had instructed the positronic brain to let us rematerialize near the orbit of Pluto.'

'Shouldn't we see how the others are getting on?' Bell asked.

'That won't be necessary,' replied Rhodan, and got up after the robots had left the room. 'The robot nurses will

9

take care of them much better than we can. Besides, why shouldn't they make it if we did?'

The visiscreen above the control panel lit up. Slowly the colors fell into a pattern and then turned into 3-D pictures. The brightly flaming star to the left side in front of the craft's nose was the sun, Bell and Rhodan recognized. Directly before them floated a weakly glowing celestial body, covered by a whitish icy layer . . . Pluto.

The hyperspace jump had been a success!

'Our Pluto base crew doesn't know our new ship yet,' said Rhodan. 'You'd better inform them at once. They might already have located us with their spacewarp sensors, or even have given the alarm.'

The spacewarp sensors were an invention of the Arkonides. They reacted over great distances to any vibrations in the four-dimensional space-time structure and could pinpoint their location. Each hyperspace jump caused such a tremor, which propagated itself faster than light and without any loss of time. Gravitation, as the Arkonides had known for thousands of years, was nothing but a five-dimensional energy radiation, which needed no time to displace itself through space.

Bell went to the transmitter to call Pluto. He used a simple set rather than the hyperwave transmitter. He wanted to make sure no unauthorized listeners somewhere light-years away would intercept his message. Fortunately for Rhodan and his men the post on Pluto had not yet relayed the news about the strange spaceship. Bell breathed a sigh of relief. He reminded the men on Pluto to remain on the lookout for any approaching spacecraft and to notify Galacto-City at once.

'We should warn Earth of our coming,' suggested Rhodan. 'Otherwise they might send a reception committee to greet us. The new space fleet should be completed by now. They might be overwhelmed at the sight of this giant of a ship. After all, our *Good Hope* had a diameter of only a hundred and eighty feet, just like the other twelve auxiliary vessels we have here on board with us. Use the hyperwave transmitter, but pinpoint the beam so that it can be received only in Galacto-City.'

With the help of the faster-than-light hyperwaves, communication with Terra was established within a few seconds. Galacto-City, Rhodan's power center on Earth, came on; but before the radio officer on duty could say anything, Bell ordered: 'Switch off your transmitter at once. Don't broadcast with hyperwaves! Now here in brief are the instructions for your commanding officer: The *Good Hope* was lost in the Vega system in a space battle between the Ferrons, our allies from the eighth planet Ferrol, and the invaders from the Topid system, a double sun more than eight hundred light-years from Earth. We won and captured a gigantic spacesphere of Arkonide origin. The Topides and the Arkonides have been at war for thousands of years. The lizard-like Topidian race rules over three smaller solar systems at the rim of the Arkonide galactic empire. The Topides intercepted the distress signal of the wrecked Arkonide space cruiser on our moon and wanted to attack Earth. But due to some miscalculations they landed in the gigantic system of the Vega sun. We arrived there just in time to join the battle. This will explain why we aren't returning with the *Good Hope.*

'You must inform all nations of our impending arrival. We'll be landing in Galacto-City in about four hours. Our spacecraft has a diameter of three thousand feet and is spherical. In order to avoid panic breaking out among the peoples of the world you must inform them that this giant is not part of an invading alien fleet but the new battleship of the Third Power. End of message. Over and out.'

In the meantime a man had come into the command center. He was tall and gave the impression of being young and resilient despite his obvious advanced age. Snow-white hair crowned his unusually high forehead under which peered out a pair of bright, almost golden eyes. Khrest, the last descendant of the ruling dynasty on Arkon, the center of a distant star realm, who had been forced to a crash landing on the Earth's moon several years ago, and who since that time had become Rhodan's ally, seemed to have gone through the hyperjump with ease. He smiled briefly.

'With this ship alone the Topides should have been able to conquer the solar system,' he remarked in the Arkonide language, which Rhodan and Bell could understand thanks to their hypno training. 'We were fortunate to seize the spacesphere without damaging it.'

'Even atom bombs can sometimes do some good,' interjected Bell dryly.

Khrest looked at him in surprise.

'I don't get you.'

'Would there be any mutants without those early atom bomb explosions? Mutants who can read thoughts and are capable of jumping halfway around the world? Would there be any human beings who possess telekinetic powers? Or to put it differently: would we even have become aware without those detonations what abilities have been slumbering in our brains for thousands of years, talents that suddenly have come to life? We have eighteen of these mutants as allies, and without their help we'd probably not be sitting in this spaceship here.'

Khrest smiled again. This time with more amusement.

'The logic of your argument is overwhelming. I submit without protest.' Then suddenly serious, Khrest added: 'I only hope that your argument will remain as valid in more important matters. So far we have not totally defeated our

Topidian enemies in the Vega system, don't forget that, my friend. It's only a hop, skip and jump (as you humans would say) from here to Earth. Unless we return in time. . . .'

'No need to worry about that, Khrest,' interrupted Rhodan with a slight smile. 'I've sent at least five messages from Vega to Earth, and all have been received in Galacto-City. I'm convinced all my instructions have been carried out. As soon as we land on Earth we'll find a well-trained crew ready waiting for us, to man the *Stardust II*. In addition to that we'll have at our disposal fighter squadrons of F.T.L. mini-spaceships, ready for battle. It will take but a few days or weeks at most to chase the Topides to the end of the universe.'

'Let's hope you're not too optimistic.' The cool voice spoke from the direction of the entrance. Nobody had noticed when Thora, the former female commander of the Arkonide expedition that had foundered on the moon, had come into the room. She too was tall and had whitish hair that contrasted strangely with the delicate tan of her lovely complexion. Her eyes were shining golden-red and flashed in a mixture of icy contempt and quiet admiration. It was just this strange mélange of her feelings that continuously attracted Perry Rhodan to this beautiful alien woman.

They had grown closer during the past few years since first they met. Yet they had never been completely able to bridge the abyss that time and space had created between them. Millennia of decades and more than 30,000 light-years lay between them. But Rhodan already felt appreciative that she had come to regard humanity as thinking beings and no longer wild primitives that should be destroyed, as she had done at first. However, Rhodan recognized the new danger that lurked behind that beautiful face. Thora had become their ally for one reason only: the Earthlings were supposed to assist her in finding a way to return to her home planet Arkon. And this moment she had so longed for had now arrived, for the *Stardust II*, the Arkonide battleship Rhodan had captured from the enemy, was the spaceship that could carry her back to Arkon.

'I doubt that I'm overly optimistic, Thora,' Rhodan replied calmly, looking straight into her reddish-golden eyes. 'Certainly, I admit that I was quite worried before we dared the hyperjump through the fifth dimension. But we succeeded. And we shall return via the same route, but this time well armed. The Topides won't find an opportunity to attack Earth. They don't even know where Earth is located in the universe.'

'Still, you must admit that you're in a bad spot,' she said with an odd lurking note in her otherwise melodious voice. 'Mankind has hardly ventured out into space and you encounter undreamed-of obstacles. In the course of a few years you've already met four extraterrestrial intelligent races. You managed to ward off a dangerous invasion of your home planet only with the help of our powerful weapons. And now Vega! For the first time, Earthlings interfere with interstellar affairs and enter an area that so far belonged exclusively to the Arkonides. Do you think that is right of you?'

'Of course I think we're right to act this way. I wonder what the degenerate Arkonide race would have done in my place? You weren't even capable of lifting your crash-landed cruiser off the moon again! We had to come to your assistance, Earthlings that had for the first time reached the moon in a liquid fuel driven primitive rocket. Don't forget that when you speak of the present conditions. If we hadn't rescued you from the moon you probably would still be sitting there whiling the time away by watching senseless abstract patterns on a picture screen.'

Khrest stepped over to Thora and put his hand on her shoulder.

'You shouldn't talk this way, Thora. We and Rhodan are friends, allies in a battle against a hostile world. He's helped us the same way we helped him. If ever we see Arkon again one day, we'll have to thank him for it.'

For a moment Thora stood motionless next to the entrance, then she lowered her eyes. As many a time previously she gave up the fight against Rhodan. This man's will was stronger than hers. But it was not only the power of logical reasoning that told her so; there was something else besides.

They had long since crossed Saturn's orbit. Jupiter became visible at the side and soon disappeared behind them. But not until they had reached the orbital path of the planet Mars did the *Stardust II* diminish her speed. Perry Rhodan prepared the ship for a landing on Earth.

The first radio messages were exchanged. Colonel Freyt, who had been in charge of the Third Power's affairs during Perry Rhodan's absence, confirmed the receipt of the hyperwave communication from the Vega system and announced that all orders had been followed.

For an instant Rhodan's and Thora's eyes met. He exchanged a friendly smile with her, without displaying the triumph he felt inside. Reginald Bell was far less considerate.

'Haven't I always told you that nothing could possibly go wrong?' he said with a great deal of self-assurance, and patted his friend Perry on the back. 'Do you want me to take charge of the landing procedures?'

'Yes, take care of everything,' answered Rhodan in an absentminded way. For his thoughts were already preoccupied with what would await them upon their arrival on Earth.

Galacto-City was filled with intense activity.

At the shores of the Goshun-Saltlake, in the middle of the Gobi Desert, had risen the gigantic metropolis of Rhodan's mighty domain. His territory was hermetically sealed off from the outside world. It formed a square whose sides were each 120 miles long. In its very center reposed the invisible energy dome which was fed by the inexhaustible Arkonide reactors. Below the center of the energy screen was the heart of the new realm, the gigantic positronic brain. Outside, strictly separated from the administrative and living quarters, stretched the long sheds of industrial plants where 50,000 specialists were busy at work. If their number had not been supplemented by an army of work robots, the extensive installations would have needed at least 500,000 workmen. Altogether 230,000 carefully screened inhabitants called Galacto-City their home.

Beyond the residential area were two regular airports in addition to a spaceport, all heavily guarded by robot troops. Three space-fighter squadrons, built on Earth, stood ready for battle: altogether one hundred and sixty-two ultra-modern fighter machines.

As the gigantic sphere appeared in the sky, even those who knew of its existence felt their hearts skip a beat. At first they noticed only a small ball that quickly grew in size. But the sphere kept getting bigger until the sun was blacked out by this new celestial body. The shadow of the Arkonide cruiser fell over Galacto-City.

The craft floated for several seconds above the energy dome before it began to drift off slowly as if it were a child's balloon. It disappeared below the horizon in order to touch down at the spaceport.

Perry Rhodan was the first to leave the spacesphere. He saw a man come toward him who was as tall and lean as Rhodan himself. He was dark-haired and approximately thirty-seven years old. Sharp lines marked his face, but some of these wrinkles revealed clearly his great sense of humor. He came to a halt in front of Rhodan, extending a hand in a friendly greeting.

'Welcome back to good old Terra! We're happy to have you with us here again!'

'Thank you, Colonel Freyt!' Rhodan smiled, grasping his friend's hand with a firm shake. 'I'm afraid, though, I'll stay here for only a short time.'

Freyt could not conceal his consternation.

'I don't understand. . . .'

Rhodan turned around and pointed at the gigantic structure made of unknown metal alloys towering up into the sky like a skyscraper.

'And you don't ask me what this is, Freyt? I really admire your self-control.'

The lines in the former officer's face seemed to grow deeper.

'Curiosity isn't one of my virtues. I suppose you'll tell me all about it in due time. Why should I bother you?'

'You're right there, Freyt. By the way, I'm just as anxious to hear your report as you are to hear mine. Bell is taking care of the disembarking procedures of the crew and their transport into town. I'll come directly with you. The meeting will take place in two hours under the energy dome. Will you see to it that all those in authority remain close by, to be consulted if the need should arise? Now, just let me know quickly if everything is all right here.'

'In perfect order, don't worry!' reassured Colonel Freyt, who was now smiling again.

An airglider brought Rhodan, Khrest and Thora to Galacto-City where they were greeted by a jubilant population.

Two hours later the meeting began of the outstanding

heads of Rhodan's Third Power, as the coalition between the Arkonides and the Terrans was generally known.

Rhodan opened the session.

'I'm pleased to note your joy at our return, but I want to tell you immediately that we came only in order to leave again as soon as possible, equipped in the best possible way. Before I give you a detailed report of our experiences I would first like to call on Colonel Freyt for his résumé.'

The colonel cleared his throat but remained seated.

'We received your hyperwave messages from the Vega system and have some idea about what happened to you there. We started at once, according to your request, with the hypno-training of two hundred and fifty specialists from the guard troop. This training has been completed successfully in the meantime. These men will become part of the crew for your new spacecraft, as you had indicated. We've also concluded with great success the special training of the mutants on our Venusian base. The mutant corps is ready for action with the exception of Nomo Yatuhin, whose telepathic abilities are not up to par yet. I've already arranged for the return of all mutants to Earth. They're back home from Venus.'

'Splendid.' Rhodan nodded with pleasure. 'Crew and mutant corps are then ready for action. How about the robots?'

'As you know, some robots were salvaged from the destroyed Arkonide cruiser on the moon. These were mainly specialists for repair work and maintenance. If you can make use of those . . .'

'Certainly, Colonel Freyt. Our new ship is immense. How far did you progress with the construction of your own spaceships here on Earth?'

'It will take us another year to complete the cruiser according to the plans put at our disposal by the Arkonides.

But our cruiser won't be as gigantic as the one you brought back to Earth with you from Vega. . . .'

'Some ship, isn't it?' interrupted Reginald Bell, sounding as proud as if he himself had built the huge spacesphere.

Rhodan did not pay any attention to him and methodically continued his inquiry.

'How are things here on Earth? Any political news? Do we finally have a united world government?'

Slowly Colonel Freyt shook his head.

'I'm afraid not yet, Rhodan. You can't really expect that age-old traditions will be overthrown within a few years. You accomplished a great deal at the time when you prevented the outbreak of an atom bomb war with the help of the weapons from your Arkonide allies. This brought about a union of all the great powers of the world. But we are still far from a regular world government, I'm sorry to say. On the other hand, something has happened that I consider to be of the same order of importance. Allan D. Mercant has succeeded in uniting all defense and secret services of the world under one organization, which is known as T.D.U., Terra Defense Union.'

Allan D. Mercant was the chief of the Western Defense and thus one of the most powerful men of the free world. He sympathized with Rhodan's cause and had come over to his side on the basis of rational conclusions.

'Well, that's at least something to be grateful for,' admitted Rhodan. 'But let me tell you now about my own plans. In the Vega system we became involved in the battles between some of the native inhabitants and alien invaders. The natives are the Ferrons from the planet Ferrol, while the invaders are known as the Topides, members of an intelligent reptilian race. The Topides succeeded in conquering the eighth planet of the Vega system; the Ferrons fled to the ninth planet, which they call Rofus. We captured the gigantic spacesphere and promised soon to return with more help. John Marshall and Doctor Haggard remained on the ice moon Iridul. That is about all.'

'Why'd you leave the two men behind?' asked Freyt, surprised.

'They've established a small base there in order to keep watch over the hyperwave transmitter of the *Good Hope*, which can no longer be repaired. In case danger should threaten Earth from any Topidian armada, the two men will warn us immediately. This is an essential part of our defense. Several Ferrons have been added to their support, and their safety on the ice moon is assured. They're living in a deep cavern in the ice and have been supplied with all necessary equipment. Iridul resembles Pluto in size as well as other conditions.'

'And now are you planning to return to the Vega system?'

'We've no choice in the matter. We're doing a favor not only for the Ferrons but also foremost for ourselves. The Topides might decide tomorrow to attack Earth; after all, twenty-seven light-years mean nothing if you're used to thinking in terms of interstellar spaceflight! Therefore we must forestall them. This is why I wanted to make sure that conditions on Earth are stable, which would permit me to have a free hand elsewhere. We shall drive the invaders out of the Vega system before the thought can occur to them to make a serious search for Earth, which they suspect to be situated somewhere in this sector of the galaxy.'

'When are you going to take off?' inquired Colonel Freyt in a matter-of-fact tone.

'As soon as the crew is familiar with the new ship. I shall personally supervise their training. Bell will be entrusted with the supreme command. And there's something else I'd like you to do. We've brought back with us many films of the battles in the Vega system and candid shots of the in-

20

vaders. Have two hundred copies made of each film and distribute them all over the world. I myself will record a running commentary for these filmed documents. I'm sure these eyewitness reports won't fail to make a suitable impression on our population of the horrors of interplanetary war. . . .'

Their success exceeded all their expectations.

People gathered in all the big cities of the world and demanded the final union of all governments on Earth. Perry Rhodan was feted as their liberator and officially rehabilitated by the government of the Western bloc. His so-called 'transgression' of having used the superior technological advances of the shipwrecked Arkonides for his own purposes was forgiven. Nobody blamed Rhodan any longer for having built up his own neutral domain with the help of the Arkonide scientific achievements rather than handing them over to the world at large.

Now Rhodan was assured that the whole world was standing solidly behind him.

But there was little time for Rhodan to enjoy his victory, for the task that was ahead of him demanded his concentrated effort. In the meantime Bell was drilling the three hundred members of the crew until they had everything pat, and they were about to drop with fatigue. It took exactly eleven days to get the crew ready for action. Bell could report that the *Stardust II* was ready for takeoff.

Four of the auxiliary vessels were supposed to remain on Earth to supply reinforcements in case of an emergency. The space that these four auxiliary vessels normally occupied in the gigantic storerooms was now available for two fighter squadrons, one hundred and eight ultrafast and supermodern machines that were under the command of Major Deringhouse and Major Nyssen. These tiny torpedo-shaped miniature spaceships accelerated within ten minutes to the speed of light.

Rhodan gave orders for a final roll call. Although Bell felt absolutely sure of himself in general, this was something that made him nervous. He had the men line up in front of the gigantic spacecraft, got busy with petty details, such as inspecting their uniforms for loose buttons and dusty boots, until a guard announced Rhodan's arrival. Major Deringhouse and Major Nyssen stood at the right wing next to their pilots.

The men were standing stiffly at attention, like toy soldiers, when Rhodan's car approached. He got out together with Khrest and Thora. Rhodan walked over to the men.

'Crew of the battlecruiser ready for action, sir!' reported Bell.

Rhodan's eyes assumed a quizzical look, as he took in the scene. 'At ease, men! We aren't in the army here, after all!' he reminded them. His remark, of course, was addressed to his friend Bell, who seemed to have taken his job a bit too seriously for Rhodan's taste. Then Rhodan took a package that he had been carrying under his left arm, and held it in his right hand. 'As I've just been informed, you're all ready for battle in the Vega sector. We're facing a difficult task; let's hope we can accomplish it. But keep in mind, the world's fate depends on our victory. If our enemies should attack our solar system, Earth would be lost. In the meantime you've become familiar with this marvelous ship and you've learned to run it and service it. As you know, the ship is equipped with weapons capable of annihilating entire planets. With this craft I'm placing a tremendous source of power into your hands. It's my wish, friends, that this power be used for peace and good causes. But let's not forget that often you have to do battle in order to preserve

22

peace and freedom. And now I'd like to ask our Arkonide friend Thora to christen our vessel.'

Rhodan had opened the package and now pulled out a bottle of champagne. Thora stepped forward, looking quite pale, and seized the bottle. Rhodan gave her a glance of encouragement. Khrest stood over to the side and stared rigidly at the giant sphere. Perhaps he was thinking that this ship used to belong to his own race, but that from now on human beings would take possession of it.

Thora walked toward the spacesphere with tiny, halting steps. She stopped short of it, lifted her right arm, hesitated for a moment, then hurled the bottle against the metal hull. Only then did she break the silence. 'I christen you *Stardust II.*'

Rhodan hurried to her side, hands outstretched. Only he could fully appreciate how hard it must have been for the proud alien woman to give the former Arkonide ship a Terrestrial name. For a few seconds their hands joined in a firm clasp. Then Thora turned abruptly and walked slowly back to the waiting car.

This very moment, Rhodan knew, he had laid the second foundation stone to the future star realm of man, who someday would take over from the decadent Arkonide Empire.

Rhodan addressed Reginald Bell. 'I'd like to take *Stardust II* out on her first test flight for maneuvers in the Asteroid belt. Khrest and I will participate as observers in this action. We should return by tonight. Our bases on Venus, Titan and Pluto have already been informed of our plan.'

The men broke rank hesitatingly at first, then everything went with lightning speed. The anti-grav lifts carried the men to their stations, escalators began to roll, bulkheads were opened and closed, air pumped out of the airlocks, generators began to hum, then the hatches were closed down after Khrest and Rhodan had come aboard.

A short while later the *Stardust II* blasted off.

Bell sat in front of the intercom and gave orders. His subaltern officers were huddled in front of similar installations that were dispersed all over the ship. Tiny visiscreens showed the men's faces. Inside the hangars the pilots got into their fighters. The cabins were shut and the air streamed out of the hangars.

While the Earth sank back underneath them in the glass-clear ocean of air like a giant rock, then became imbedded in the blackness of space, Rhodan began to issue commands.

'Fictitious attacker has occupied Jupiter. Outpost on the Asteroids. Enemy plans to attack Earth. Our goal: to destroy the outpost and counterattack on Jupiter.' Rhodan looked at Bell. 'Carry on from here!'

'OK,' promised Bell, and rattled off instructions into the microphones. Then, while the *Stardust II* accelerated to the speed of light within the next ten minutes, going up to 50,000 G's, Bell leaned back in his chair, folded his arms in front of his chest and inquired casually: 'Sir, would it please you if I were to pulverize Jupiter while we're at it?'

'You'll forget your silly jokes when things get serious and we really attack the Topides someday,' prophesied Rhodan. 'Well, how about it? What are the men doing now?'

The silly grin left Bell's face. 'I'm not joking, Perry. In less than an hour our fighters will have turned several asteroids into fiery gas clouds and thus annihilated any supposed enemy hiding out there. Then the fighters will set course for Jupiter and attack all enemies trying to flee from there. With this ship it would be entirely within our power to change the giant planet's surface into a flaming hell.'

'That really wouldn't be necessary, but – I don't want to

interfere with your plans here. Carry on!'

Bell was now in his element. He proceeded with great skill. Nobody would have suspected such talent in him. Although the automatic steering mechanism relieved him of having to navigate the giant sphere, all initiative and strategical planning were left up to him.

The *Stardust II* raced into the Asteroid belt, then slowed down. The first fighter squadron left the hangars and swarmed into space. Deringhouse was in constant radio communication with Bell, who kept naming imaginary targets and then had them attacked by the fighters. Rhodan followed the maneuvers on the visiscreens. Khrest stood next to him, not saying a word. A secret fire was burning in his golden eyes but no gesture revealed his innermost thoughts. Only Rhodan had some vague idea what was taking place now behind the Arkonide's high forehead.

Finally the *Stardust II* descended low over Jupiter's surface, racing across the dead planet, shooting at imaginary targets indicated by Rhodan with lightning speed. Where just a moment ago had been ice-covered terrain, now boiling lava-lakes could be seen. The fighters under Deringhouse's command paid brief visits to the planet's inner moons, then reported as having destroyed the imaginary enemy forces stationed there.

Rhodan put his hand on Bell's shoulder. 'You can sound the retreat now, Reg. I'm satisfied with this maneuver. I believe we can feel reassured when we return to the Vega sector. I'm full of confidence now. We've recouped our loss of the *Good Hope* a thousand times over with this space-cruiser. The Topides had better start looking out.'

For the first time Khrest broke his silence. 'It would be easy for you to destroy the invaders,' he said pensively. 'But I wouldn't recommend it. You cannot prevent all enemy ships from fleeing the battle scene and then reporting to their home base what happened. There are counter-weapons even against the best equipped battleships. The Topides would think of nothing but revenge till they were ready to return someday and take up the fight again. It would be wiser to come to an agreement with them.'

'A peace treaty with those lizards?' pondered Bell.

'Why not? The intelligent races of the universe come in many different shapes; that doesn't mean they're better or worse than we are. The Arkonides have concluded friendly deals with spider-type creatures. Our best friends belong to an aquatic race living in the oceans of a watery world. No, my friend, the outer appearance is not what matters. Only character should count.'

'Do the Topides have any character?'

'Everyone has a character,' replied Khrest seriously. 'Sometimes the character is good, sometimes it's bad. That's the only difference.'

'What do you suggest we should do now?' asked Rhodan. 'Propose a peace treaty?'

Khrest shrugged his shoulders. 'Let's return to that question later – once we meet up again with the Topides. They might be willing to enter into negotiations after they've suffered a defeat.'

'There's something else I'd like you to answer for me,' said Rhodan, looking Khrest straight in the eye. 'What do you think of my crew here? Do you believe they'll prove themselves in an interstellar conflict?'

'You can rest at ease,' replied Khrest, trying at the same time to suppress the admiring look in his eyes. 'What I've witnessed here today is like a dream from the glorious past of my Arkonide ancestors. That's the way we were way back when we started to build up our galactic empire. Today, unfortunately . . .' For a moment he was silent, his face betraying the embarrassment he felt. Then he smiled and continued bravely: 'You could be the direct descendants of the former Arkonides.'

While Bell issued commands for the fighters to return to the mother ship, Rhodan remarked as if lost in thought: 'Perhaps that's what we are – speaking figuratively, of course.'

Chapter Two

THE KEY TO ETERNAL LIFE

Forty-two planets revolve around the bright star Vega. Intelligent life developed only on the eighth planet. The Ferrons were a short people, rarely taller than five feet four inches. Their eyes were small and deepset, their foreheads bulging. Their copper-colored hair and pale-blue skin – a result of solar irradiation – formed a strange contrast. Their tiny mouths made them appear harmless. The climate on their home planet Ferrol was hot and tropical. Their short, thickset bodies were perfectly adapted to the 1.4 G's of their own world.

Many Ferrons, however, were no longer living on Ferrol. After the invaders occupied their homeland, many of them fled to Rofus, one of the planets they had colonized. There they settled down, waiting impatiently for their liberators, the Arkonides, who had so suddenly appeared from nowhere and dealt the Topidian enemy a crushing blow.

The Ferrons had in their possession matter transmitters, capable of operating throughout five dimensions and over tremendous distances. Yet they had not progressed very far in their knowledge of space flight; they had not mastered five-dimensional mathematics either. These two facts seemed to be inconsistent and Rhodan was rather puzzled by this.

An ice-moon revolved around the twenty-eighth planet. The satellite's former atmosphere had become precipitated eons ago and changed the moon's surface into an icy desert with high mountains. No life could exist in this hellish climate. Still, Iridul was far from being a dead world.

Hidden deep inside one of these mountains there was an immense cavern whose smooth walls still bore signs of recently molten rock. A wide tunnel led to the moon's surface. An airlock permitted John Marshall and Doctor Haggard to leave the cave anytime they wished aboard one of their two fighter planes, in order to carry out reconnaissance flights.

The foundation of the hyperwave broadcast station was expertly camouflaged in the eternal ice. Nearby were the plastic living quarters of the two men and their Ferron companions. Generators provided light and heat; an air-conditioning system made life bearable beneath the frozen surface.

John Marshall, a natural telepath and member of the mutant corps, was preparing for a reconnaissance flight. Haggard, the famous hematologist from Australia, assisted him in his preparations.

'I miss Bell,' said John wistfully. 'I'm really looking forward to seeing his silly grin again.'

'What loneliness won't do to some people,' kidded Doctor Haggard. 'Wherever Reg shows his face, you can bet that Perry, Khrest and Thora won't be long in putting in an appearance. That's what's probably at the root of your nostalgic feelings.'

'Yes, especially Thora,' admitted John, and adjusted the transmitter in his helmet. 'What a woman!'

'She's colder than all the ice of Iridul!' Doctor Haggard pretended to shiver with cold. He grinned. 'If you should as much as entertain the thought in your wildest dreams . . .'

'Don't worry, Doc. I wouldn't poach on Rhodan's territory.'

The physician watched silently as Marshall climbed into the cockpit of the plane and closed the hatch behind him.

Haggard stepped over to the switch-panel next to the hyper-wave sender and depressed a lever. At the same time he activated the regular wireless set to keep in touch with the pilot.

'All set?' asked John.

'You can start. Good luck!'

'Thanks.'

The fighter took off suddenly on anti-grav skids, gliding along the brightly lit tunnel.

The airlock gates closed behind it. Pumps began to hum. Then the door to the outside world opened up ahead. John moved the joystick, and the tiny machine, its cabin just large enough to accommodate one person comfortably, shot out into the dim sunlight.

Vega was much too far away to cause the glittering ice crystals of this small satellite to sparkle properly. The wide snowy expanses reflected the light coming from Vega and other stars, but only because of the total lack of any atmosphere on Iridul. The shadows stood out starkly and formed an uncompromising barrier between darkness and light.

John climbed slowly, hardly accelerating. He rose leisurely up into the star-studded sky, enjoying the view. His eyes searched for a certain constellation he knew from back on planet Earth. He located it almost immediately. The contours had shifted somewhat, and an entirely new star stood almost at the center of the familiar picture. The star shone yellow and not too bright: the sun, Sol, twenty-seven light-years away. John had just turned four when the light he was seeing this very moment had started on its long journey through space. In the meantime, John had over-taken the sun's rays. And now they met up again.

I've seen the same light now for the third time, thought John. *Extraordinary! Unique! Is it at all possible to see the same light more than once?*

He couldn't pursue these philosophical speculations further, that never led to a tangible result anyhow, for something aroused his attention. At first he wasn't even aware what it had been, but then his brain began to work: no star could move as fast as that. No planet either. And there are no glowing meteors moving through empty space.

A spaceship?

He turned his fighter plane around and accelerated. He wasn't afraid of being attacked. He knew he could pick up speed much quicker than any enemy ship. Long before they could get ready to charge, he would have fled to safety. John couldn't exclude the possibility that the invaders might have recovered in the meantime from their terrible defeat. He was sure the loss of the gigantic spherical cruiser had been rough on them – but they still had left a battleworthy fleet of faster-than-light spaceships.

Another flash of light!

John switched on the search-robot, which at once activated its reflecting rays. Seconds later the fighter's nose moved slightly to one side and pointed directly at the slowly approaching star.

Here it was! A Topidian ship!

The magnification magically produced a shadow on the screens. At once John recognized the circular bulge around the center of the slender spacecraft. This was a dead giveaway for a Topidian vessel.

John deliberated, but with lightning speed. It would make no sense to tangle with the enemy. Rhodan had forbidden all attacks on the Topides, and given orders to avoid any encounter with them until he returned with the *Stardust II* and an effective fighting force.

All the same, it was interesting in itself to note that the Topides had resumed activity again. They apparently had wanted to secure their position of power in the Vega system and therefore had set out on a scouting mission to the outer planets. There was no danger that they would become suspicious of Iridul, however.

John changed course once more, with a heavy heart, and sent a brief report to Haggard in order to warn him. It would be advisable from now on not to leave the protection of the underground cavern.

John accelerated with a tremendous thrust of power and soon reached the speed of light. Otherwise it would have taken days to get to the ninth planet, considering the colossal extent of this system.

Rofus reminded him vividly of Earth, except for the absence of big cities. The Ferrons had settled on this planet a long time ago. They were more than happy now to use it as a place of refuge. A sufficient number of natives had remained on Ferrol, mainly the Sichas, an almost wild tribe of brave warriors. They lived in the mountains and had given the Topidian invaders a very hard time.

John intersected the orbital paths of several planets and slowed down his fighter when the eleventh planet passed by in the distance. In a few more minutes he sighted the ninth planet. He orbited around it several times to make quite sure that no enemy scout planes were nearby. Then he landed in Tschugnor, the capital of Rofus.

Almost daily John or Doctor Haggard flew to Tschugnor in order to visit the Thort of Ferrol. The ruler of Ferrol had fled to safety from the Topidian invaders. His ministers and collaborators had followed him into exile. He resided in Tschugnor and via matter transmitter he kept in constant touch with his secret agents who had remained on the home planet, now occupied by the enemy lizard race. Radio communication had been discontinued and the spaceships no longer left their secret underground hiding places. Ferrons and news capsules traveled between the eighth and ninth planet via the same system that had enabled the *Stardust II* to execute her hyperspace jump. No one, however, knew the secret of these artificially constructed teleport installations. John was quite certain about this.

Normally no one paid any special attention to the Terrestrial visitors during their periodic stays on Tschugnor. But there was something special in the air today, John noticed, as he climbed out of his craft. He shut the hatch and switched on the electronic barrier. Anyone coming too close to the ship would receive a painful jolt. The barrier reacted only to John's brainwave pattern.

The streets of the city were bustling with activity. John became aware that many Ferrons were busy transporting all kinds of heavy loads. He tried to learn telepathically what was going on, but in vain. The only impressions he managed to receive were so confusing that they were less than useless for him. He merely perceived vague generalized fear and worry, that gradually began to upset him in turn.

What had happened?

He made his way to the Thort's residence as fast as he could. He was admitted at once and soon sat across from the ruler of the Ferrons.

No vestige of his former royal dignity could be discerned in the little man. He simply grasped John's strong hands as if pleading for help. John understood him, due to his telepathic abilities, and could dispense with the usual translating robot; he even managed to answer him in a more or less intelligible fashion.

'Sir, our lives are in jeopardy,' began the desperate Thort. 'Unless the great Rhodan is going to help us we'll all be lost.'

'Rhodan is already on his way.' John lied in order to calm down the little man. 'What's happened? You act as if the Topides had started an offensive on Rofus.'

'An attack is imminent. Till now they've kept quiet on Ferrol, but now we hear nothing but reports about preparations going on that can only lead to the conquest of Rofus.'

'Do you have positive proof of that, or do you just suspect it?'

'We're absolutely convinced. According to our agents' reports the lizards' fleet is getting ready to attack Rofus. Many of my subjects on Ferrol have been arrested, imprisoned and even killed. The Topides have gotten over their initial shock of Rhodan's sudden appearance on the scene. Now they're bound to come here to take vengeance. That means we'll have to suffer for something we haven't done at all. The Arkonides are obligated to come to our assistance now.'

Fine thanks we're getting for our help, John thought. *Gratitude doesn't seem to be their strong point.*

'Do you have any clues as to when this invasion is supposed to come off, Thort?'

'No, no definite clues. But it can come any day. And all we have left of our defensive forces is our badly mangled fleet.'

'That wouldn't be of much help,' John admitted thoughtfully. He sensed that the time for action had come. Rhodan had left him behind to keep an eye on any further activities of the Topidian enemy here. In case they had really overcome their shock and renewed their attacks, it was John's duty to give immediate alarm. Rhodan would have to interrupt the training of his special crew and start at once. John had no idea how long it would take the huge battle cruiser to traverse the distance of twenty-seven light-years, but it should not exceed a few days, at most. No doubt it was his duty to send off the prearranged signal and to inform Rhodan.

34

'I must have valid reasons, Thort, to request Rhodan's presence here.'

'Isn't it sufficient proof that the Topides are getting active again? Until now they didn't budge and stayed quietly on Ferrol. But now they've resumed regular patrol missions throughout the entire system.'

True enough. John himself had seen such a patrolling vessel in the vicinity of the twenty-eighth planet.

He rose. 'All right, Thort. I'll send a message at once to Perry Rhodan to return here in a hurry. Keep your fleet ready for action. It's quite possible that you'll have to ward off the enemy's first blow all by yourself. Go ahead and train troops that can be transported to Ferrol via the matter transmitters. They're to create diversionary actions behind the enemy lines. Once Rhodan arrives here, we'll strike the decisive blow that will finally chase these reptilians out of the Vega system for good.'

'Let's hope we'll survive long enough to see all this come true,' sighed the ruler. He didn't seem too convinced by this likelihood. But then he drew himself up to his full height, holding his short squat stature as erect as possible. His tiny mouth became a thin line, giving his face an air of determination. 'We will and we must beat the Topides. I must liberate my oppressed people on Ferrol. Even if many managed to escape here to Rofus, the best people have remained behind!'

A few minutes later John was on his way back to his fighter plane. He walked on foot in order to gather some more impressions and also to be able to think about his talk with the Thort. He could never quite figure out these Ferrons. True, they had progressed far enough to develop space travel, but they had never gone beyond the initial stages. They had colonized the seventh and ninth planets but their ambitions had stopped short there. Yet they knew a way of dematerializing matter and even themselves and then transport all over tremendous distances. Via the fifth dimension! Without any loss of time! For this one needed technical and mathematical knowledge. And the Ferrons quite obviously lacked those. John was certain they were even unable to build such a transmitter. These machines had been handed down through generations; they must have originated in the far distant past. The story of their origin had been lost. They were the remainder of some period of splendor, a highpoint of technological excellence that had vanished.

Or had the Ferrons once been in contact with a superior civilization from whom they had obtained these transmitters? And had that civilization fallen into oblivion?

John found no answers to his questions and no longer pursued this train of speculative thought. He knew that Perry Rhodan had been puzzled by this problem too but had not arrived at any conclusions. Maybe this was the key to a secret whose solution would answer many questions.

Suddenly it was much easier for him to divine the thoughts of the Ferrons who were hurrying past him. They were fleeing. They were leaving the city to seek refuge in the mountains before the enemy's impending attack.

John found his fighter exactly the way he had left it. He removed the barrier and took off without delay. Shortly after leaving the atmosphere of Rofus, he accelerated to the speed of light and set course for the twenty-eighth planet. Vega shrank rapidly and lost its brightness.

Once again he detected another spaceship with his position finder but it was too far away for direct sighting on his visiscreen. He didn't doubt for a single moment that it was another scout ship of the Topides.

He cautiously circled around the twenty-eighth planet several times before he landed on the moon Iridul. Doctor

Haggard was already waiting for him and opened the air-lock.

Two minutes later the pilot climbed out of the cabin and announced: 'We must send the message, Haggard. The Topides are resuming their activity. I'm convinced it's high time to chase them out of this system.'

'Rhodan's orders are to use the hyperband sender only in case of emergency – we risk detection, you know. Fortunately nobody can determine for whom the message is intended. And Earth's position must remain a secret.'

'But it must be sent. Get everything ready; I'll compose the text of the message. It must be brief and still say all that's necessary.'

Doctor Haggard nodded in agreement. 'I'll make it in about ten minutes. By the way – two hours ago we made an instrument sighting of a Topidian ship. It was orbiting around Iridul as if it were looking for something. Is there any connection with the things you've been able to find out?'

John could hardly hide his consternation.

'You bet there is,' he said quickly. 'A great deal, even worse than I thought. Hurry up, we'd better not waste a second. Scout parties may be harmless, but they're usually the forerunners of far less harmless events later on. I'm afraid the Topides are preparing to take possession of the Vega system.'

Doctor Haggard switched on the current. A dull roar suddenly filled the wide cavern. Lamps started glowing. The gigantic sender began to vibrate, sending waves to Earth without any loss of time, for one light-year meant for them as much as twenty-seven light-years. Indeed, exactly the same as 32,000 light-years – and there was the snag.

Throughout the universe receivers would be registering these waves.

Position finders might even indicate that the sender could

be found somewhere in the Vega system. But since this system was not part of the Galactic Empire, it would probably arouse curiosity. Someone might decide to investigate this situation and see which race had reached and surpassed the technical pinnacle of normal progress by penetrating into the fifth dimension.

A red light flashed.

'All set,' said Haggard, and pointed to the tiny cabin just large enough to accommodate one person. 'Go in and read out the message. You have exactly thirty seconds. Then the message will be repeated automatically.'

'You know,' remarked John with a forced smile, 'whenever I see this sending cabin I'm reminded of the matter transmitter the Ferrons are using. Both this cabin and the matter transmitter have certain things in common: the Ferronian apparatus transports human beings through hyperspace, while we do the same thing with our waves. I always have the uneasy feeling that someday things might go wrong; we might have a misconnection and I, rather than my words, might land on Earth.'

It was a strange thought, but Doctor Haggard didn't treat John's words as a joke. 'It's not as improbable as you might think, John. The only thing that really worries me would be the location in which you'd materialize again. After all, there are many receiving stations in the universe!'

John's face grew pale, nevertheless he entered the cabin with a determined step and shut the door behind him.

The hum increased; he began to speak.

Perry Rhodan received the report a few minutes before takeoff. Colonel Freyt, who had already taken his leave and had stepped off the *Stardust II*, returned in a hurry and brought the text. This message didn't change anything in principle, it only intensified Rhodan's determination to clear

38

up the situation in the Vega sector as fast and as thoroughly as possible.

'Thanks, Colonel Freyt. We intend to be back within a few weeks, if everything goes according to plan. In the meantime, I hope you'll do all you can to bring about one united government on Earth. The time for racist differences should by now have become a thing of the past. Mankind can assume the role of heir to the Arkonide Empire only after having become truly citizens of Terra. Do you see my point?'

Freyt faced Rhodan squarely. 'Of course I do. Now, my friend, goodbye and lots of luck.'

After Freyt had left, Rhodan stood in the ship's command center for a moment as if lost in thought. Reginald Bell walked over from the communication console and remarked with a frown on his round face, 'It would be a smart idea to let on as little as possible to Khrest what you intend to do – I mean about being heir to the Arkonide Empire. He might not take too kindly to the idea.'

To his surprise, Rhodan reacted with a smile. 'That's where you're wrong, my friend. It's Khrest's secret desire that one day we'll take over from them as masters of their Galactic Empire. He realizes only too well the old regime will founder without us. Thora is the only one who refuses to listen to reason. But enough of these dreams of the future! Is everything ready for lift-off?'

'All set.'

'It's high time we start. The message from Iridul sounded very alarming. The Topides are getting ready to attack Rofus. We must forestall their plans.'

'Our mutant corps will show them a merry dance,' promised Bell, returning to his place at the control board.

Colonel Freyt stood motionless at the edge of the field as

the huge spaceship lifted off silently, then shot up into the clear sky like a gigantic missile. A few seconds later he lost sight of it. He sighed and climbed aboard the glider that took him back to Galacto-City.

A difficult task lay ahead of him.

This time everything went smoothly with the transition. The ship slid into hyperspace, traversed the fifth dimension and materialized at the edge of the giant Vega system. They established radio communication with Haggard and Marshall, who breathed sighs of relief when they learned that now their exile on the ice moon Iridul was coming to an end.

'Reg, order one fighter squadron to take off and go on ahead. The Topides don't need to know where we're going to land. I want to conceal the position of the *Stardust II*.'

'Where's the ship supposed to touch down?' asked Bell, after he had carried out Rhodan's command and had passed on the instructions to Deringhouse. 'On Iridul?'

'No. On Rofus. It's a better base of operations. I also believe that the danger is greatest for the ninth planet.'

'Why don't we attack Ferrol directly? We can certainly risk it now with the *Stardust II*, don't you think?'

'I have my reasons for not doing it that way. No sense in establishing our rule by an unnecessary show of violence. I'll be satisfied when the Topidian lizards scurry off helter-skelter, convinced that it's useless to offer resistance against us. I want them to be panic-stricken whenever they think back to their adventure in the Vega system.'

While the small, easily manageable space-fighters left their hangars and hurried ahead of the giant sphere, flying in close formation, Haggard and Marshall came aboard the *Stardust II*. Their Ferronian allies remained on Iridul for the time being. Rhodan extended a cordial greeting to his friends.

'I'm anxious to hear further details from you now,' he said after the first excitement of the reunion had died down somewhat. 'Your radio message was very brief. What happened?'

'Not very much until now, but the Thort grew restless. He felt deserted, even betrayed. But then I managed to regain his confidence and he followed my suggestions and assembled a small battle fleet. With it he succeeded at least to beat off a slight attack of the Topides that was probably intended to test the Ferrons' strength and resistance on Rofus. Still, it was quite a morale booster for the Ferrons, even if it wasn't much of a victory. I'm afraid, however, if ever the Topides should make any serious attempt . . .'

'It must never come to that,' interrupted Rhodan. 'The lizards will soon find out that we've returned. Our fighter squadron received orders to carry out diversionary actions, so that we can land on Rofus without interference. Do you know if they have an underground hangar there big enough to shelter the *Stardust II*?'

'I would think so,' answered Marshall. 'But – are we going to hide out again? I had hoped we'd let those reptiles know who's master here.'

'You bet your life we will.' Rhodan smiled, then glanced quickly in Bell's direction. 'Why do you think we brought along our mutant corps? Though our friend Reg isn't one of them, he still has some surprises up his sleeve. Under his guidance our mutants will make life so unpleasant for the Topides that they'd rather roast in hell than stay here any longer. Or maybe they'd even prefer freezing to death in deep space.'

'I'm going to—' began Bell enthusiastically, but Rhodan cut him short.

'Hold your horses, old pal. Let's wait till we've landed safely on Rofus, then we'll discuss this matter further. Right now concentrate on evading the Topides. Watch those detection finders!'

'I won't miss a thing, not even spacebugs,' kidded Reg, and turned away to devote himself to his task of surveillance. He no longer paid any attention to Rhodan and Marshall, who resumed their discussion.

'Any further news?'

'Not really, Rhodan. Except for one thing that worries me. I shouldn't say "worry", to be honest, but rather that it makes me wonder.'

'What is it?'

'The Thort,' said Marshall slowly. 'I've talked a great deal with him and had plenty of opportunity to probe his thoughts. He's honest, that's true. And he's even grateful for our help. But there's one area that he's kept secret from us. It has something to do with the matter transmitter.'

'Hm,' murmured Rhodan. 'What's he trying to conceal from us?'

'Something he doesn't know himself. I know this sounds odd, but it's the truth. The Ferrons haven't developed these transmitters on their own.'

'I thought so, my friend. But it's interesting to find out that the Thort himself is aware of that. What else could you read in his brain?'

'There's a sealed vault on the planet Ferrol. Five-dimensional locks keep everyone out. Only the Thort knows how to open these locks, without understanding their purpose. This knowledge seems to have been passed on from generation to generation since time immemorial. I get the impression these transmitters were a gift from an alien race, who in the distant past had received some great favor by the ancestors of our Ferrons. This vault is supposed to contain the exact plans for the construction of these transmitters. The Thort was thinking of studying these plans in order to build some.'

'That doesn't surprise me either,' remarked Rhodan without apparent emotion. He noticed Marshall's disappointed expression. 'I wasn't trying to be facetious, John. You've rendered me a tremendous service with this report, for now you've confirmed what I'd suspected earlier: the Ferrons could never have invented these five-dimensional transmitters, for they lack the necessary mental prerequisites. Now, I'd like to know, who did build them?'

'I got a tiny hint on that, too,' replied Marshall with a radiant smile. 'I could sense the Thort was thinking of something like "beings that live longer than the sun". Does that make sense to you?'

These words had a startling effect on Rhodan. And Bell, who by now was tuned in on their conversation, suddenly sat up stiffly in his chair near his instruments. First his face grew unnaturally pale, which was followed by a deep blush. His eyes flickered. He slowly turned to Rhodan and met his friend's eyes, which were also wide with amazement.

Marshall observed with great interest the effect his report had evoked; he smiled with contentment.

'What an unusual pleasure to make you lose your cool!' he chuckled. 'That alone has made my lonesome stay on Iridul worthwhile. Now I feel amply rewarded. Indeed, these creatures that live longer than the sun have given the Ferrons the secret of the matter transmitters eons ago. I'm sorry to say that they didn't know too well what to do with this secret.'

'The Ferrons are thinking in four dimensions, and that's already a giant step ahead, as far as we're concerned. It's just that they don't think five-dimensionally. And that's the first prerequisite if you want to construct hyper-spaceships

43

or matter transmitters. That alone was enough for me to realize that the Ferrons could never have built these marvels themselves. Tell me, Marshall, could you get some indication where these beings reside who are supposed to live longer than the sun? Where are they located?'

'Somewhere in the Vega system,' replied Marshall. And for the second time he experienced the thrill of seeing Rhodan lose his composure. 'At least that's where they were several thousand years ago, when the Ferrons were still in touch with them. Unfortunately, that's all I could make out, by probing the Thort's brain. I believe he doesn't have any further information on that.'

For several minutes Rhodan sat silently in his chair and stared at nothing in particular, while his thoughts were racing ahead. Beings that live longer than the sun, he thought. How long does a sun live? Half a day, because it rises in the morning and sets at night? A year, because every planet in a solar system needs one specific year to complete one revolution around the sun? Two hundred million years, the time it takes for the sun to revolve once within its galaxy? Or longer still? An eternity? Do these beings have eternal life? Did they not know death? But – if this should be the case, why did anyone never meet them?

He sighed.

'We'll have to have a talk with the Thort, once all this is over. I'm now intrigued more than ever with the secret surrounding this matter transmitter. And where is this crypt you mentioned earlier supposed to be, Marshall?'

'In the underground vaults of the Red Palace on Ferrol. And only the Thort knows where the entrance is.'

'Well, the Thort!' mumbled Rhodan. 'He's the key.'

Bell looked up. Marshall asked: 'The key? To what?'

'The key to eternal life,' Rhodan said softly.

Admiral Chrekt-Orn, Topidian commander-in-chief on the conquered planet Ferrol, was sitting at his desk in the Red Palace. His face bore an expression of grim determination, the thin lips of his broad lizard snout were firmly pressed together. There was a nonstop flow of alarming news. Rhodan's space-fighter planes, under the command of Deringhouse, had rushed several light-hours ahead of the huge Arkonide spacesphere, embroiling the Topidians in mock fights and luring them to the other side of the Vega sector.

An assistant adjutant entered the room. 'Strong fighter units have appeared in the vicinity of the ninth planet. We're hot on their heels. No attack was attempted by the enemy; they beat a hasty retreat at the first sign of interception. No casualties to report so far.'

The admiral, resplendent in his colorful uniform, hit the table with his clenched fist.

'I don't care whether the enemy is attacking us or not! I've given express orders to wipe out any hostile force that dares show their face in this sector!'

The adjutant tried to proceed cautiously. After all, it wasn't wise to incur the wrath of one's superior in general. But especially not under the circumstances, since Chrekt-Orn had been empowered by the almighty ruler of the Topides to act on his behalf here in this foreign land. He could mete out any punishment he pleased. The adjutant defended himself: 'The moment we set course for these tiny ships, they begin to accelerate and take flight at incredible speeds. We had no luck so far even destroying one of these fighters, let alone capturing one. Our technicians would be most eager to find out something about the power-drive they use.'

'It's of the Arkonide type,' the admiral murmured bitterly. 'The same as in our lost Arkonide battle cruiser. Have you found any trace of it?'

'Not yet, Admiral. Nobody, not even our spies on the ninth planet, have been able to get the slightest hint where it disappeared to. It seems to have simply vanished from the fourth dimension.'

'Could be,' growled Chrekt-Orn. He was furious. 'Could very well be. Then we might never see it again. That wouldn't be bad at all. How could we defend ourselves against that battle cruiser, especially if it fell into the hands of an intelligent enemy? As far as these small fighter planes are concerned' – now his voice resumed its usual sound of authority and energy – 'we should make short work of them. I expect reports of successful sorties in the very near future. Pass this on to the commanders of our battle squadron groups. There'll be honors and rewards for the victors.'

However, neither threats nor promises would work.

The lizards tried in vain to catch the agile fighters, those daredevils who would come close to the heavy cruisers, then avoid them with lightning fast maneuvers, luring them farther and farther away from Rofus.

Meanwhile Bell set the *Stardust II* down on Rofus, undetected by the Topides. The giant spacesphere was placed inside the immense cave of a newly created hangar that ordinarily could accommodate entire squadrons. Rhodan issued his commands, and ten minutes after completion of the landing procedures he was sitting opposite the Thort, who displayed visible signs of relief at the sight of Rhodan.

'I'm most pleased that you've responded so quickly to my request for help,' the Thort said at the beginning of the meeting with Rhodan, Khrest, Thora and Marshall. 'The Topides are about to invade our world here. We don't know how to fend them off. You, with your spacesphere . . .'

'We're going to defeat the enemy without even deploying our battle cruiser,' Rhodan remarked calmly. He paid no attention to the Thort's startled reaction. Rhodan continued. 'I've brought a special group along with me. They're all born on my home planet. From now on they'll carry on the fight against the enemy. Within a few days, or weeks at most, you'll be able to return to Ferrol.'

'My battle forces are at your disposal,' offered the Thort.

'Thanks. I'll make use of them when needed. I really neither plan nor foresee any open battles against the enemy forces. If we should be forced into this kind of action, I'll certainly not avoid it. But it's my intention to let as many Topides as possible escape and return to their home world in order to report what kind of a reception they got here when they tried to conquer your part of the Vega system. That should cure them for good of their lust for conquest. At least in this region as well as in our Sol's system.'

'Sol?' the Thort asked with eager curiosity. 'Is that what you call your sun?'

'Yes,' replied Rhodan, who had made notice of the Thort's sudden show of interest. 'That's our sun, indeed.' Rhodan quickly changed the topic. 'Are the matter transmitters still working all right? Are you still transporting people to Ferrol?'

'We've maintained communication with the Sichas. All is well in Sic-Horum. Kekéler leads the resistance on Ferrol.'

'Excellent,' said Rhodan. 'That's where we'll start, then. What we began to accomplish when we conquered the Arkonide battle cruiser, we'll finish off right here. We'll break the enemy's resistance at the very root.'

'What do you mean?'

'I mean to say that I'll be sending my people right away to Ferrol. Today, in fact. Reg, you'll be in charge of this mission. Any suggestions you wish to make, Khrest?'

The Arkonide scientist slowly shook his head.

'I have a notion of what you intend to do, and I can't think of any better solution. Your mutants are the right people to frighten the Topides enough to last them a lifetime. I fully agree with your plan, Perry.'

Rhodan glanced at Thora. She just nodded briefly to indicate her approval.

'All right then,' Rhodan said with satisfaction. Then he turned to the Thort. 'Will you, please, put several cars at my disposal to bring my mutant corps to the matter transmitters. I'll oversee this action myself, and Reginald Bell will be in charge of any further activities. Reg, you know what to do, don't you?'

'I can vaguely figure out what you want from me,' admitted Bell with a faint grin. 'I'm sure I can cook up something.'

'I wouldn't doubt it, my friend.' Rhodan chuckled in amusement at the thought of Bell's ingenuity. Rhodan rose from his seat, bringing the short meeting to an end. 'By the way, Thort, I'd like to learn all the details about the events ages ago on Ferrol. I'm sure you have documented reports of your nation's history.'

The Thort's healthy blue complexion turned to a sickly grayish blue. He stared in bewilderment at Rhodan. His little mouth remained half open as if he were trying to get out the answer that had gotten stuck in his throat. Now a hectic flickering passed over his face. John observed the Thort very attentively. His probing thought-feelers penetrated gingerly into the Thort's brain, endeavoring to register its impulses. But he found only surprise and consternation. Then, finally, the Thort spoke up. 'Our history? What could you find of interest in my people's history? What connection could there be with our present war against the Topides?'

'Maybe nothing, and maybe a lot, Thort. So how about it? Can I study your nation's past or do you want it to remain an eternal secret? And if so, why?'

'No,' stammered the Thort, still overwhelmed by Rhodan's sudden request. 'Why should I want to conceal my nation's past history? We're friends, and friends don't hide things from each other. You reveal your home planet's galactic position and I, in return, will tell you about our past.'

'Also about those creatures that live longer than the sun?'

This time even Rhodan was shocked at the sudden change that fell over the Thort. The grayish blue tinge of his face became almost white. Something akin to fear and awe filled his restlessly darting eyes. He started trembling all over.

'How do you know of them?'

'I just do.' Rhodan dismissed the question with a negligent flick of his hand. 'How about it, Thort? Are you going to tell me about these beings and where they live?'

The Thort simply shook his head.

'Even if I wanted to tell you, I couldn't do it. It's too far back in the past, and our reports have grown hazy with the passage of thousands of years. I'm willing to procure all available data. Then we can continue our discussion. I hardly believe, though, that I can be of real help to you in this matter.'

'I'm sure you'll greatly assist us, Thort.' Rhodan sounded amused. He reminded his friend Reg, 'Let's not waste any more time. We've waited too long already.' Then, speaking again to the Thort: 'I shall remember your promise. This isn't a whim on my part. If these beings do indeed live longer than the sun, they still ought to exist today. For the sun is still with us.'

Kekéler stepped out of the matter transmitter cage on

Rofus. An urgent message from Rhodan had called him to the ninth planet. Rhodan, Bell and the mutant corps welcomed the Sicha, who was dressed in the colorful garments of his people.

'I'm happy to meet our allies again,' began Rhodan. 'And how is the liberation movement progressing?'

'It's cost us many victims, but we haven't really made any progress,' admitted Kekéler sadly. 'The Topide lizards get more and more suspicious of us. They've dismissed nearly all native help from their services. They've doubled their guards everywhere. We've established communication with several resistance groups, and our organization has improved. But this step ahead is evened out by the severity of the Topidian methods of reprisal. Only the other day, they destroyed one of our villages, killed off all its inhabitants, because they suspected them of hiding one of the resistance fighters.'

'Just like back on Mother Earth, not too long ago,' muttered Rhodan bitterly. 'Go on, Kekéler! Any news?'

'None, Rhodan. We'll continue fighting until the Thort can return to Ferrol, or until we . . .' He hesitated. Then he swallowed hard and added: 'We'll all be dead.'

'Don't worry, friend. This will never come to pass. I've brought reinforcements with me. Some members of the mutant corps are already known to the Sichas. Tako Kakuta, for instance. And you'll probably remember Wuriu Sengu. But whatever their names, they're your friends, of both the Ferrons and the Sichas. The headquarters of the resistance groups will be moved to Sic-Horum, the capital in the mountains. From there, Bell will deploy his forces as needed.'

'Everything has been prepared for your arrival,' said Kekéler.

'Thank you. Bell and I have discussed all the details of

this action, and he's fully informed. I'll arrive in Sic-Horum three days from now and take charge of the final stages of the battle of liberation. And now – farewell! Good luck!'

Kekéler hesitated for a moment. Then he gathered up his courage. 'We need weapons, Rhodan. Without weapons . . .'

'Weapons?' Rhodan acted surprised. 'Oh, I almost forgot to mention it. We won't need any weapons anymore. From this day on, we'll fight the invaders with one kind of weapon only: our brains. And I know we have better brain power than the lizard race.'

The door of the matter transmitter cage opened. The first of the mutants stepped inside.

Chapter Three

'TO LIVE LONGER THAN THE SUN'

Trker-Hon sat across from his commander-in-chief, Admiral Chrekt-Orn. The two beings, descendants of a reptilian species, were covered with gray-black scales and presented a nightmarish sight. Their broad frog-like faces, their thin-lipped snouts, their black protruding eyes, their flat skulls and their nonhuman extremities – all of these together contributed to make them appear in an unsympathetic light to the human eye. The Ferrons too felt the same repulsion to the appearance of these creatures that had invaded their home planet. The lizards presented a visual impression of cruelty – but even worse: they were of a truly cruel character.

'Our offensive will start tomorrow,' said Chrekt-Orn with some emphasis. 'We must assume the Arkonide battleship has become the victim of some accident. Most likely, the Ferrons didn't know how to operate it properly and have vanished for good in hyperspace. Thus our chances have increased to win a speedy victory over this race and to take possession of the entire system. This way we should also find that ship which sent a call for help and originally brought us here to this part of the universe.'

'Sometimes it seems to me,' mused Trker-Hon, 'we might've made a mistake and landed in the wrong system. You can't exclude the possibility of a miscalculation when dealing with such big distances.'

'Our Despot's technicians never commit an error!' declared the admiral firmly, reminding his subaltern that a superior doesn't fall victim to the same frailties as other mortals. 'This is the right system, and we're going to locate the stranded Arkonide cruiser. We have to find a replacement for the one we've lost. Or do you really even consider returning home without your ship? You know what fate would await you there.'

There was no doubt in Trker-Hon's mind what to expect in such a case.

'Our Despot is a fool!' volunteered Trker-Hon. 'He's cruel and stupid besides!'

The admiral looked at his adjutant with amazement. He was perplexed and utterly confounded. A hissing, whistling sound escaped his lips, giving expression to his feelings of utmost bafflement. His scales were rattling and changing color.

'What did you say?' he yapped, gasping for air. No one had ever dared to make such offensive remarks about the exalted ruler of the Topides. He would have to place this young man under arrest, have him court-martialed. Only one punishment would fit this abominable crime: death! 'What did you say?' he asked again.

'And you're a fool yourself, Admiral! Don't you see the wrong we're doing here? These natives are a friendly harmless people, who are entitled to rule over their own home planet. What right do we have to come here and take over their world? I'll say it once more: you're a big fool for carrying out the Despot's orders without ever questioning them. This blind obedience won't free you from being held responsible for your actions at some date in the future when you'll be brought to trial.'

The admiral tried to smooth his unruly scales. Never before had he encountered such outrageous behavior. Never throughout his long career had an officer rebelled in his presence. The man must have lost his mind.

'Trker-Hon! I'm placing you under arrest!' The admiral pushed a button and waited for an orderly officer to enter the room. 'Hjera, call a guard! Trker-Hon's been stripped of his rank. He'll be court-martialed.'

'Are you mad, man?' said the orderly. He didn't budge, made no move to comply with Chrekt-Orn's orders. The admiral couldn't believe his ears; he was thunderstruck. The world seemed to come to an end for him. His race had known only blind obedience since time immemorial. The slightest rebellious attempt had always been stamped out ruthlessly at the very first sign. And now this!

He sounded the alarm. Armed guards stormed into the room, holding their dangerous deathray guns ready to shoot.

'Arrest these two!' gasped the admiral. He was breathing hard. 'They're making insulting remarks about our Despot. They must be brought to justice! We'll punish—'

Words failed him as he crumpled in his seat. He was too old to have to put up with such monstrosities. Silently, the guards disarmed the two evildoers, whose faces suddenly reflected nothing but utter surprise. They offered no resistance when the guards led them away. Trker-Hon and the orderly officer seemed merely baffled. 'What's all that supposed to mean?' wondered Trker-Hon aloud. But he didn't receive an answer to his question.

That was merely the beginning of the offensive campaign the mutants were waging against the Topidian lizards.

Bell had put back in operation the one-man matter transmitter inside the Red Palace. Thus he was able to send his men, individually, straight to the central command post of the Topides. The cage of the receiver was concealed in a secret chamber, built between hollow walls which had not yet been discovered by the enemy. A narrow corridor ran along between the hollow walls, branching off in many places, and led to various rooms, chambers and passages. This was most convenient for Bell's men to pop up suddenly anywhere in the Red Palace and to disappear just as swiftly. The former builders had really thought of everything, though certainly they never suspected that their prudent foresight would play a vital role someday in driving off invaders from their home planet.

Wuriu Sengu was once again the key figure. He and Bell were sitting together in a corner of the hollow wall, as he put his amazing gift into action. The short, squat Japanese had a round face and black, bristling-stiff hair. He was the 'seer' of the mutant corps. Solid matter presented no obstacle for his eyes. He could see through everything and was able to recognize any object on whose atomic structure he would focus his special vision. The moment he changed focus, the object became invisible again to his eyes.

'What's going on?' Bell whispered eagerly. He was thoroughly enjoying this guerrilla warfare right in the middle of the lizards' headquarters. He had an innate desire to make things as complicated as possible in order to increase his enjoyment. This prevented him from letting loose his mutants on the enemy's army to cause them to mutiny. He wanted to squeeze every drop of pleasure out of this whole enterprise. Those lizards should shiver with fright for the rest of their days whenever they'd think back to this military expedition.

The Japanese whispered in return: 'The admiral had both the officer and the orderly arrested just now. André Noir did a good job here.'

A chuckle came from the opposite corner, where the Frenchman was sitting. He had been born in Japan and was one of those types who radiated their good-natured temperament for miles around them. He was known as a 'hypno' and could impose his will on others. Not only on human beings, but also on animals, extra-terrestrial creatures and alien intelligent life forms. He had just given renewed proof of his remarkable ability.

'Wow, that's fun! I've just released this Trker-Hon from my hypnotic spell. Of course, he can't remember a thing. He can't understand why the general had him put under arrest.'

'Admiral,' corrected Sengu.

'What's the difference, Sengu? The main thing is the lizard chief will see discipline collapse all around him. He won't be able to figure this out and he'll start doubting his own mind. Better still, he'll gradually begin to believe in ghosts.'

'He'll hardly be able to avoid that.' Bell grinned. 'I hope their entire army will soon believe in ghosts. That's what Rhodan wants them to do.'

Sengu kept staring at the wall.

'The two guards are taking their prisoners to jail and are locking them up. I'd like to know what the admiral's next step will be. I wonder if he'll have his best collaborator condemned to death.'

'Topidian morale won't leave him any other alternative,' said Bell. 'What crazy creatures!'

'Why?' asked André Noir in a serious tone. 'I haven't forgotten the time when we had similar conditions back on Earth.'

'Hush!' urged Anne Sloane, who had kept silent all this time. The dainty American girl was a natural telekinetic. Thanks to her special gift she was capable of lifting and moving any object across tremendous distances just by concentrating her mental powers. Sengu was clasping her right hand in his strong fist. Thus she could perceive anything he saw. By combining their various talents the mutants could multiply their potential many times over and thus increase their usefulness and heighten their chances of reaching the optimum of their effectiveness. 'The admiral seems to be getting over his shock. He's speaking on the communicator now. Of course, I can't understand what he's saying.'

'But I can,' said Noir. He was clasping Sengu's other hand. Only Reginald Bell sat in his corner, unable to see anything, for he was not one of the mutants. 'He's giving orders to call a meeting for the discussion of a special military operation. All the battleship commanders who aren't presently engaged in encounters with the enemy are being invited. At the same time he's issued orders to get the hyper-wave band senders ready. After the meeting he wants to establish direct communication with the Despot on Topid. Wow! That's over eight-hundred light-years away. I can't wait to listen in to that!'

'He isn't fed up yet, I hope. . . .' Bell was afraid he might be cheated out of all this fun. He sounded so disappointed that Anne couldn't help laughing. 'I wanted to scare the living daylights out of him before he . . .'

'Don't you worry,' interrupted the Frenchman, full of confidence. He could appreciate Bell's concern. 'On the contrary, he wants to obtain the Despot's permission to abandon the eighth planet and at the same time official sanction for annihilating Ferrol. And then he said something else before he switched off the communicator. He mumbled some words to himself. I don't quite see what he meant by that.'

'What were those words?' demanded Bell. He was suddenly very serious.

'It sounded like: "The wrong world . . . but I'll still find the right one."'

'He meant Earth,' growled Sengu, the Japanese mutant. 'Does mankind live longer than the sun?'

Bell sat up straight as a bolt. 'What? What did you say?

57

Say that again!' He could hardly talk, he was so excited.

André Noir smiled triumphantly. 'Did I finally get a rise out of you? I can't believe it! Yes, that's what the admiral was muttering to himself. Something about the right world, whose inhabitants live longer than the sun. Is that of any significance?'

'Rhodan will be most interested to hear of that.' Bell resumed his usual casual tone. He relaxed in his seat in the corner. 'When will this meeting take place?'

'Within the hour. Afterward, the talk with their home planet Topid.'

Bell was fumbling with the tiny communico-set he was wearing on a bracelet around his left wrist.

'They're in for something! And they won't like it!' he growled angrily. He seemed to have forgotten that this was going to be a fun thing.

Admiral Chrekt-Orn entered the conference room and all the assembled officers fell silent. Chrekt-Orn sensed the tense atmosphere and could literally feel the deep resentment directed against him.

He saluted briefly and asked them to be seated. Then, as if this were the normal thing to do, the admiral's scales lost their color, he started to crow strangely – a sound totally unfamiliar to the lizards' ears. Now the admiral spread out his arms, fluttering and waving, then ascending effortlessly up to the heavy chandelier where he settled comfortably between the arms of the light fixture. From this vantage point he looked down upon the utterly consternated officers and began his address: 'Gentlemen! Our enemies the Ferrons use the most abominable means to break our rule. Just a few minutes ago I had to witness how Trker-Hon uttered the vilest insults against our exalted ruler. He called him a fool, which is putting it mildly, in my opinion. I would've used much stronger words to express my feelings. Therefore

I had him arrested and shall condemn him to death. After all, it's not possible . . .'

That was as far as he got. Somebody emitted a shrill whistle and ran out of the room. Several of the officers followed suit. An elderly stouthearted officer seized the chance he must have been waiting for a long time.

'Silence!' he shouted at the top of his voice. 'The strangers who came to the Ferrons' assistance are using black magic. Don't get confused! Remain calm and rational, follow my example. We must fight against the enemy. . . .'

This was the end of his speech. He was fully conscious, like the rest of the Topidian officers in the room, for André Noir didn't conjure up an illusion this time. It was the real thing. Suddenly the ground fell away from beneath his feet and he sailed up to the ceiling toward the admiral, who was crouching anxiously in the chandelier. Soon both lizards were sitting in the tiny space, clutching at each other desperately. They stared in amazement, with ruffled scales, at the chaotic scene down below.

The officers who had remained in the conference room had seen enough. Their superiors were in league with the bad spirits and were out to ruin them. Better to fight against the Ferrons; they were easy game in comparison. They were real and could be defeated. They fled headlong out of the room. Only the admiral and his senior officer remained, waiting anxiously for someone to get them safely down from the ceiling.

Hardly one hour later, and eight hundred light-years away, the exalted ruler of the Topides received a detailed but quite confusing report of the events in the Vega system. He issued commands to hold out on the occupied planet at all costs, until the already alarmed committee of investigation would arrive. He nominated a new commander-in-chief of the occupied territories in the Vega sector and gave him full mandatory powers.

The new commander-in-chief, Rok-Gor, started his career with the order to attack Rofus with a strong battle force. They were to wipe out all Ferronian troops stationed on that planet.

Unfortunately, this was a mistake, for it only hastened the development of the events that would prove to become fateful for him and his race. Of course, Rok-Gor had no way of knowing that.

Back in his hiding place Bell was shaking his head energetically.

'No. Rhodan's ordered to leave them strictly alone. Let them proceed with their attack. Deringhouse and his fighter squadron have been alerted. Ras Tschubai is with Deringhouse. How these two can stand it inside that tiny cabin is a mystery to me. But I've some idea of what's going to happen; I can imagine what their plans are.'

He was wrong, though, for what really took place was beyond his rather vivid imagination.

Deringhouse sat at the controls of his small craft, whose cabin was just large enough to accommodate one person comfortably. Ras Tschubai, an African, was a big man. He sat cooped up at the other end of the cabin and tried to look out of the porthole. He managed to get a good view of the largest part of the surrounding universe. Ras was one of the teleporters of the mutant corps; he could transport himself to any place he desired by concentrating on it, provided he was familiar with it or could see it directly with his own eyes.

Deringhouse was in direct touch with Rhodan via the central station on Rofus. Thus he learned of the approaching fleet which had orders to attack Rofus.

The other fifty-three machines of his squadron remained in loose formation and made constant sorties designed to lead astray any possible Topidian advance patrol vessels. Deringhouse's forces were located exactly between Rofus and Ferrol.

Trker-Hon, who had been released in the meantime, led the Topidian battle fleet. Though he couldn't make sense of the latest events, he tried to shake off the secret fear that gripped him. He was determined to eradicate the source of all this calamity, which he believed to be on Rofus. Of course he couldn't guess that this source was – of all places – located in their own headquarters.

The twenty hump-bellied cruisers emerged from the shadow of the planet Ferrol and journeyed forth into the bright splendor of the Vega system.

The Topidian direction finders located them at once and Trker-Hon gave orders to attack.

Trker-Hon was half sitting, half lying behind his instrument board and stared out of the wide visi-hatches at the hated opponent whom he knew to be faster than any Topidian ship. It seemed therefore all the more surprising to him that these fifty vessels made no attempt whatsoever to escape. Was it their intention to make a stand in the face of a concentrated attack of his twenty heavy battle cruisers?

Trker-Hon kept up constant communication via TV with the commanders of the other cruisers. A hopeful note was in his voice as he issued commands for a slight change of course which marked the beginning of the attack on the hostile forces. He'd give hell to these Arkonides or to their friends who looked just like them and surely were at least of a related race. As far as he was concerned all of them were Arkonides and thus belonged to that race which tried to rule the universe, a task to which only the Topides were entitled.

The first officer of the flagship entered the command

center. The instant he reached the middle of the room in order to make a report to the commander, something very strange happened. Trker-Hon was able to see it clearly. He'd just turned around at the sound of the approaching officer.

The airspace near the officer began to waver as if it had been suddenly heated up. Something pushed the first officer aside with a sharp jolt – and then became visible. Ras Tschubai materialized right in the middle of the enemy's command center, immediately next to the Topide officer. He was grinning from ear to ear, amused at the fright he gave the two reptilian enemies. Their eyes protruded even farther than normal. Their scales began to rattle ominously and jutted out at a right angle from their leathery skin. Then the scales changed color, going from pink to a light green.

Ras removed the raygun from the belt of the stupefied first officer. Ras pointed the gun at the instrument board. He appeared perfectly composed, as if this were nothing unusual he was doing here. He pulled the trigger. The fine energy stream turned the glittering instruments into a glowing dripping mass of useless matter which evaporated as a result of the tremendous generation of heat.

Trker-Hon didn't comprehend a thing, but he acted instinctively. With one mighty jump he leaped from his seat toward the black ghost. But before he could lay his hands on him, the stranger had vanished into thin air. Only the raygun fell, clattering to the metal floor. The commander and his first officer were once again all alone in the demolished command center.

Ras Tschubai displaced himself to another part of the big battle cruiser, jerked several big guns from their holds, made the totally perplexed Topide crew take to their heels, opened the airlock and dematerialized.

Trker-Hon noticed at a glance that the intruder's shot

had destroyed only some unimportant instruments. The communication with the other ships of his fleet was still intact. He managed to shut the airlock just in time. But the opened airlock made him think. Had the black creature left his ship via the airlock? That would mean it could survive in the vacuum of space!

A cold shiver ran over the pointed scales on his back. Then this couldn't have been an Arkonide, but a member of another race. This might explain their mysterious powers!

He looked out of the visi-hatch and saw that the little enemy ships kept at the same distance. Regardless whether the Topidian ships tried to come nearer to them or to get away from them, the distance remained unchanged. Trker-Hon called the other cruisers: 'Set course for the ninth planet! We'll carry through with Rok-Gor's commands. The right wing . . .'

He stopped short. He couldn't get out the words. Something happened on the small visiscreen which showed the command center of the seventh battle cruiser. It was the same event that had taken place a few minutes earlier in his own command center.

The black ghost materialized behind the commander of Number Seven. Trker-Hon was incapable of shouting a warning to the unsuspecting Topide, he was too fascinated by the event that unfolded before the eyes of most of the other commanders, since Ras had landed right before the lens of the televideo apparatus.

Trker saw how the ghost – or whatever the apparition might be – tapped the officer on the shoulder. The Topide jerked around; he wasn't used to such disrespectful behavior. He was chilled with terror at the sight of the black ghost. He couldn't move.

Now Trker-Hon found his voice again. 'The raygun – kill him!' he croaked. 'Quick!'

Even if the commander of Ship Seven heard Trker's warning shout, he didn't react to it. He sat halfway turned around in his seat, immobilized like a hypnotized rabbit.

Ras Tschubai grinned and walked to the instrument board. He pulled a few levers at random, pushed several buttons, turned some switches. The commander's eyes followed his movements. He didn't budge; he was unable to move.

While Ras was in the process of dematerializing in order to reappear in Ship Number Three and terrorize its crew in the engine room, Ship Number Seven began to respond to the changed settings of controls. It seemed to have gone crazy. It took off vertically, separating from the tight formation of the fleet, started to execute abstract figures, diving, rolling, turning and banking in all kinds of crazy angles. Finally it spun off sideways, guns blazing wildly, in the direction of the bright Vega star. Trker soon lost sight of it. He no longer received any answers to his urgent calls.

There was no time even to ponder about this puzzling incident. Something even more incredible took place.

The tiny hostile space fighters began their attack. They flew toward the Topidian fleet like bats shot out of hell, almost colliding with the heavier and not as easily maneuverable cruisers, creating havoc among the ships' formation. They then retreated lightning fast, only to take up their game anew a few minutes later. They didn't fire a single shot.

And then it happened.

Cruiser Number Thirteen moved up to the front of the formation, turned sideways, pointing its heavily armed broadside menacingly at the ranks of the fleet, blocking their way. Now the face of the commander of Ship Thirteen appeared on the visiscreens of the other cruisers.

'I've assumed command over the entire fleet! Return to Ferrol! Turn about! Fire!'

Before Trker-Hon could make any sense out of this mad move, Number Thirteen's heavy ray cannons opened fire, blasting pale bundled energy rays away at the rest of the formation. All protective energy bubbles surrounding each of the cruisers effortlessly absorbed the sudden bombardment. Except for Cruiser Number Nine, that apparently had switched off its force field for an instant. It disappeared. In its place, a slightly phosphorescent cloud was drifting off into space, its sharp outlines soon growing fuzzy and gradually totally fading away.

The rebellious Cruiser Number Thirteen, however, closed rank again as if nothing untoward had taken place. There was no comment, no explanation from its commander, except for his inquiry a few seconds later as to where Cruiser Nine had vanished.

Trker-Hon was trembling all over. He tried to give an answer. He realized that the officer on Number Thirteen had not acted of his own free will. He hadn't gone stark staring mad all of a sudden. No. He'd succumbed to the same evil forces that had almost managed to ruin him and his career. These Arkonides must have at their disposal powerful means beyond anyone's imagination.

Just then, at that very instant, with fading awareness, he could barely perceive the foreign mind now penetrating his own brain. But this time it was quite different from before. This time he didn't lose consciousness completely; a small fraction of it remained awake. Although he'd been robbed of his ability to make decisions, he was still capable of understanding the strange, inexplicable thing that had taken possession of his brain – even if he failed to comprehend it.

'We can destroy you,' said an inaudible voice that he could hear only inside his head. 'And we will destroy you, unless you abandon this senseless fight. Turn back at once, Trker-Hon! Report to your commander-in-chief Rok-Gor about your unsuccessful attack on Rofus. Withdraw from the Vega system or none of your ships will ever see your home planet again!'

Trker felt the pressure recede. His analytical mind returned. He stared at the mike of his videocommunico-set. His claws shot out and grasped it. He called his commanders with a croaking voice: 'Proceed with attack on Planet Nine! Let nothing deter you from the execution of my orders. And if I should issue any commands to the contrary . . .'

This was as far as he got. He felt the strange mind enter his brain again, completely blocking out his own awareness. Everything went black in front of his eyes. But this interruption lasted only a single second. Then he continued to speak, with the same croaking voice as before: '. . . I'll do this for very compelling reasons. Such as now. We're turning back to Ferrol immediately and abandoning the fight. Is that clear?'

It was far from clear to anyone. But true to their racial conditioning, the fleet made an about-face, setting course for Ferrol. There was no one as furious about all this as Trker-Hon himself when he later stood in front of Rok-Gor, unable to supply a satisfactory excuse for his inexcusable action.

'All right then,' nodded the commander-in-chief, staring at the ceiling. 'Report this incident to the investigation committee that is due to come within a few days. We've already been informed of their impending arrival.'

It was like a scene in a grotesque monster movie. The new commander of the Topidian forces, Rok-Gor, was sitting at his desk, scratching the synthetic top with his sharp claws, doodling intricate patterns. He was extremely nervous, for this was the day they expected the investigation committee from Topid.

Chrekt-Orn, now dismissed from his post as commander-in-chief, and Trker-Hon sat on the other side of the desk. Using Chrekt's eyes and ears as a meduim, Ralph Marten, the mutant, became a witness to this preliminary discussion.

Ralph Marten was the son of a German father and a Japanese mother. He'd inherited his father's tall stature and light-blue eyes, and his mother's black hair. His ability to penetrate other persons' minds and spy undetected on their actions was not a normal characteristic shared by his parents and handed down to him. This was the result of the increasing radioactivity of the Earth's atmosphere, which caused mutations in the parents' genes, later expressed as startling new talents in their offspring. Thus Ralph Marten, the mutant, could see and hear with the lizards' eyes and ears and follow their conversation. Meanwhile Ralph's body was lying rigidly in the secret chamber of the Red Palace, watched over by Reginald Bell and other members of the mutant corps.

The three Topidian lizards behaved in a rational and intelligent manner – a notion often proposed in times past by writers of imaginary stories, but which had seemed utterly fantastic and unbelievable scarcely ten years earlier. The lizards were not too much at ease in this strange environment, but they'd adjusted to it fairly well. They had different types of furniture on their home planet Topid, to be sure, designed for their reptilian body shapes. Still, here they made do with the furnishings they'd appropriated from the human-like Ferrons.

'It was nothing but hypnosis, remote control hypnotic trance!' wheezed Trker-Hon, trying to explain the reason for both blunders he'd made. First he'd insulted the Despot, then he'd withdrawn his fleet in the midst of battle. 'I wasn't aware of what I was doing. I was no longer master of my own mind. They must have machines which control other people's brains.'

'And how do you account for the fact,' Rok-Gor asked, 'that Chrekt-Orn could suddenly fly like a bird, that a black ghost appeared from nowhere right in the command center of the battle cruiser, demolishing many instruments? Was that also due to hypnotic commands?'

Trker didn't reply. What answer could he give? Chrekt-Orn, the former commander-in-chief, tried to advance his opinion of the nightmarish events. 'Our enemies must be aided by strange powers, unknown to us. We've learned from our conquests of alien races that they frequently possess incomprehensible abilities and characteristics for which we later have found some explanation. I'm sure this will be the case here too. Tomorrow the Commission will . . .'

'That's exactly why I've asked you to come here,' interrupted Rok abruptly. 'We all realize that we'll be held responsible if the campaign should prove to be a failure. And that's what it'll turn out to be in case the Commission orders us to retreat. This simply mustn't happen! We have until tomorrow to find some explanation for what's happened, and we must also find a method to prevent any further repetition. I'm counting on you for some suggestions, since you've already gathered some experiences in this field that might prove helpful.'

'Sorry. I wouldn't be of much help. I simply don't remember anything,' admitted Trker. 'I had completely lost consciousness; I have no memory of it. What could I possibly say about it then?'

'Nonsense!' Expressing his anger, Rok swept aside a heavy chair with a single blow. 'There are experts on the Commission who can extrapolate from the slightest clues.

According to experience, then, they'll leave the courier-ship only when direct contact has been established with Topid. So the Commission isn't going to fall into a trap without noticing it. Our people back home will witness the investigation directly because the TV cameras will record the picture and beam it to Topid through hyperspace. We have until tomorrow to find a satisfactory solution, otherwise the invasion will be canceled or we'll be dismissed. In either case this will mean the end of our careers. I believe we understand each other.'

'It was actually a mistake to demand that the investigation committee should come here,' Chrekt reproached. 'If we hadn't, I would still be commander-in-chief and we would've found a way out. There are no ghosts and . . .'

The word stuck in his throat. With protruding eyes he stared at the chair in the corner, where it had been lying since Rok knocked it over. As though guided by invisible hands, the various parts began to reassemble, then the structure floated slowly upward, where it hung just below the ceiling and above the new commander-in-chief. Rok followed Chrekt's startled glance upward to the chair, which was supported as though by ghostly hands, at which time the floating chair suddenly lost its invisible support and fell to the floor like a shot.

Rok didn't react quickly enough.

His mind was still in a state of shock at the impossible sight of the airborne chair and he was struggling to comprehend how such a thing could be when the gravity-defying object crashed down on his hard head, its legs draping themselves around his neck like a collar.

Trker and Chrekt regarded their superior with a mixture of horror and satisfaction, their superior who was frightened into immobility. In the meantime, Ralph Marten, through barely moving lips, whispered his account inside the hidden chamber. Bell squatted in his corner and grinned; it was very easy for him to imagine it all. Anne Sloane breathed a sigh of relief when she was able to release the chair.

'By the Gods of the Despot!' hissed Rok, clearly frightened. 'What was that?'

'The chair—' said Trker. 'The chair's taken vengeance because you kicked it. Dead things come alive and . . .'

'No!' Chrekt-Orn spoke. 'It's nothing but a trick. An illusion that we . . .'

'You call that an illusion?' raged Rok, and tore the remnants of the chair from his neck and threw them furiously on the floor. 'I have a bump on my head. Since when do illusions leave bumps?'

'I didn't mean it that way,' said Chrekt, trying to pacify the angry Rok. 'What took place here was certainly no illusion. But dead objects don't come alive. The aliens can influence our brains over great distances and they can move objects. Whether they do this with the help of machines or completely by the power of their minds, I couldn't say. . . .'

Rok shook his head in desperation. 'That's nonsense! The Arkonides aren't magicians!'

'Then maybe their friends are. Or can it be that we're confronted by two or maybe even three opponents? The Ferrons, the Arkonides – and someone else. And this someone is capable of – magic.'

'Impossible! We can't face the Commission tomorrow with such old wives' tales or we'll be washed up. A super powerful opponent, all right; that they'd recognize. But ghosts and magicians? No! This would be no acceptable excuse for the failure of an invasion. Besides, we haven't yet found the Arkonide cruiser that sent out the emergency signal. I'm almost beginning to believe too that we made a mistake with this system.'

'This star has forty-two planets,' Chrekt reminded him.

'There are a few more surprises ahead of us. And now I'd like to make a suggestion concerning the Commission we'll see tomorrow: you've dismissed me as commander-in-chief – all right, I accept that, under the circumstances. But now you too suffer under similar difficulties. We must stick together or we'll all be destroyed. So I'm in favor of your informing the Commission tomorrow that you made a mistake, that the magic's come to an end. As soon as the examiners are through with us again, we'll renew our energies against the Ferrons and Arkonides, to finish them off. . . .'

'. . . And these magicians!' interjected Trker. Rok threw him a disapproving glance but said nothing. Expectantly he looked at Chrekt but Chrekt had nothing to add.

'Is that all?' Rok's voice was full of disdain. 'You probably want to end the war at my expense! No, I'll report the truth to the Commission, so that they'll recognize our difficulties. I don't care what happens to you. The only important thing is that we find the Arkonide cruiser and the race of eternal life.'

Chrekt nodded slowly, but he caught a lightning swift side glance from Trker, who obviously didn't intend to become a victim either of Rok's lust for power. It was evident that the high command of the lizards was no longer in agreement.

'For tomorrow,' Rok-Gor went on, 'the fighting will be discontinued. I want the Commission to be presented with a muster inspection. We'll show the Despot that we too can face unforeseen events. I expect that you'll execute my command with the usual precision. Anything else?'

The meeting came to an end, but only because Ralph Marten decided to return to his friends. His body moved and he sat up. He opened his eyes and stared into Bell's intent face.

'Well?'

'Let's wait till tomorrow, Bell. I think we can do quite a few things there. Let's not forget that the ruler of the Topides will be watching.'

Bell grinned broadly.

'I'll think of something.'

In Sic-Horum, the capital of the Sichas, Perry Rhodan received the reports of his people and of the Ferronian agents. Gloktor, chief of the resistance groups against the Topides on the occupied planet, spoke in his curt, dry manner. In his outer appearance he resembled the humans, even if his mouth had turned out a bit too tiny. Deep lay the clever eyes in their deep sockets. His skin coloration was like that of all Ferrons, bluish because of the effects of the Vegan sun. Hair covered his head and half his face.

'The groups in Thorta have become more active. In the past three weeks alone four guard posts of the Topides were wiped out and at least twenty captured. Two transport vehicles were destroyed by explosives.'

'Excellent.' Rhodan nodded, satisfied. 'And what's the Topides' reaction?'

'They've finally let all their servants go and no longer give any work to Ferrons since they regard them as too unreliable. This has, of course, certain disadvantages. . . .'

'. . . Which we'll sufficiently make up for,' interrupted Rhodan. 'You probably know that we have eyes and ears everywhere.'

'I've heard about it.' The Sicha grinned amusedly. 'Everywhere they talk about it in Thorta; they say the place is haunted. However, the ghosts are on the right side.'

'They are indeed. Thanks, Gloktor, that'll be all. You'll continue your activities, giving the enemy no rest. May I ask Kekéler for his report now?'

Kekéler was the chief of the war-loving Sichas who lived in the mountains of Ferrol and had always gone all out for the unity of the planet. Despite his age and his seemingly grouchy behavior, he was very devoted to Rhodan and would've sacrificed his life to help him rout out the lizards.

'The enemy's getting nervous,' Kekéler said calmly. 'The actions of our resistance groups have already caused two of the Topidian military bases to be vacated. Since then they've been occupied by the official military forces of the Ferrons. The achievement's great. The news trickles through to us only slowly, so I'm not able to give a long and detailed report, but I know that the days of the enemy on Ferrol are numbered.'

Rhodan nodded approvingly, then looked at Bell, who was waiting impatiently for his chance to speak.

'And how about the mutant corps, Bell?'

'They're driving the lizards crazy!' The words fairly burst out of him and he looked around triumphantly. 'They're shooting at each other! – making life difficult for each other, don't get along with each other anymore! I'm planning a show that'll finally finish them off. It'll be beamed directly to Topid via TV so that the Despot can participate in it in person. Such an interesting TV play he's never seen before!'

'I wouldn't doubt that,' Rhodan agreed. 'But you mustn't exaggerate, under any circumstances. We'll discuss further details tomorrow. All the mutants will be at your disposal then. Your actions must be impressive but must give no clues as to their origin – that's very important. I'd like to mislead the Topides.

'I'm returning to Rofus now. Bell, you'll accompany me. Kekéler, you make all preparations for tomorrow's action. To confuse the Topides even more, a squadron of my space fighters will arrive here today. They'll keep the surveillance forces of the enemy busy – our opponents mustn't be given any time to think.'

Rhodan and Bell returned to Rofus via matter transmitter. It never ceased to be a strangely macabre experience to enter the wire cage, adjust the instruments and release the mysterious mechanism. Nothing seemed to happen. One simply stepped out again a few seconds later, but in the meantime had passed through many millions of miles in a dematerialized state. The transmission was through a super-ordinate paraspace, a dimension that required five-dimensional thinking in order to understand it. This mental ability the Ferrons didn't possess, therefore—

Rhodan sighed as once again his reflections led him to this point. Anyway, the Thort had promised him definitely that he'd be able to talk undisturbed with Lossoshér, the leading scientist of the Ferrons. The sage old man was a member of the council of ministers and was known as one of the wisest heads of the present generation.

'It'll depend on our conversation with Lossoshér,' Rhodan said to Bell, 'what course your performance will take tomorrow. However, I'm afraid that the Thort's set certain limits for the scientist. But with the telepath Ishy Matsu present, I'll be able to get brief data. You know, I'm sure, that she's been trained to the extent that she can transmit thought information to nontelepaths. So right while Lossoshér's talking to us we'll have the opportunity to know whether he's lying or not. We'll even know what he's *thinking* in reality at the same time, should he lie to us.'

'Stupid situation,' grumbled Bell, as they drove by electri-car to the temporary palace of the Thort. 'We help these guys and they distrust us.'

'We must try to understand that,' Rhodan said in defense of the Ferrons. 'What we want to find out from them concerns an age old historical event that survives only in their tradition. It's something that's been handed down through generations and I assume that details are no longer known. But I know that this event which took place thousands of years ago has something to do with the matter transmitters, and must have been both of a pleasant and disagreeable nature at the same time. The Thort will make every effort to keep me from finding out about it in detail – if indeed there are any details at all to find out about.'

'You mean to suggest that somebody once upon a time made a present of the matter transmitter to the Ferrons?'

Rhodan nodded.

'That's exactly what I mean to say. And I'd like to know who did it.'

The car came to a halt and the two men got out. Ishy Matsu, the dainty Japanese girl, awaited them as pre-arranged. And ten minutes later they were already seated opposite Lossoshér.

The old scientist nodded pensively.

'The great Thort reported to me what it is that you wish to know. I admit it's a delicate subject, but our common fight against the Topides has made us friends and we ought not to have any secrets from each other. The Thort's given me permission to tell everything I know about the origin of the transmitters.'

'Thank you,' said Rhodan, and listened inside himself. Ishy communicated with him: *He speaks the absolute truth.*

Rhodan continued: 'I realize that the Thort expresses great confidence in us with his willingness to cooperate. The transmitter's a puzzle because it demonstrates with its technical execution alone the incredible genius of its constructors. I'd like to know why the present-day Ferrons are no longer capable of building new transmitters. The Thort gave me some plans before my flight to Sol but they were worthless; they merely contain some clues pointing to a certain secret.'

Lossoshér replied, 'The Ferrons have never been able to build the transmitters by themselves.' This news came as no surprise to Rhodan. 'It was an alien race, to whom we once were able to render a great service. They made a present to us of a large number of mysterious instruments and included the instructions for building them. But we're supposed to be able to build transmitters only when we've reached the necessary technical and ethical maturity. Therefore the plans themselves are in a vault in the Red Palace on Ferrol, protected by five-dimensional locks and a five-dimensional force screen. It's entirely impossible to penetrate this vault unless one is capable of thinking five-dimensionally and can thus find the keys to it. These are the precautions taken by the race that made this precious gift to the Ferrons. Thus the might of the transmitters can never be misused, for only those can construct them who have the required maturity.'

Ishy, unnoticed by anyone but Rhodan, telepathed to Perry: *He is still speaking the absolute truth.*

Wishing certain conjectures confirmed, Rhodan asked without hesitation, 'Who were these strangers?'

Lossoshér smiled kindly and his gaze wandered off into the distance. It was as though he wanted to look back thousands of years in order to conjure up once again the events of the past.

'At that time we didn't have space travel yet and we stood at the very beginning of our history. But we realized we weren't alone in the universe, for we received visitors from – outside. First, a gigantic sphere landed here, but the exact story got lost through the ages – today we no longer know what really took place. The encounter was without consequences; the strangers left us again and never returned.

That must have occurred between ten and twelve thousand years ago. We surmise that the first visitors from space served as models for some of our gods.'

'Very similar to conditions on our home planet,' whispered Bell, but no one paid any attention to him.

'Then came the second visit,' the Ferronian scientist continued. 'It differed in several respects from the first. The most important thing probably was that the visitors didn't come of their own free will but made an emergency landing on Ferrol. Through that, as a consequence, came about a contact that probably had never been intended. The ship of the strangers, a gigantic cylinder, smashed to pieces in the mountains of the Sichas and was destroyed by fire, the survivors abandoning it just in time. Almost all of the travelers were saved. Our ancestors, who initially thought them to be the gods who had landed here previously, received them hospitably and later brought them the raw materials they requested to build a mysterious apparatus which would make it possible for them to return to their homeland. You're right, if you guess these to be the matter transmitters. The strangers knew no other way out, for all their radio instruments and other means of communication had been destroyed during the catastrophe.

'Then, one day, the strangers disappeared.'

'And the transmitters remained behind?'

'Yes. But earlier, the leader of the unsuccessful expedition enlightened our Thort of that day. They originated from our system and came from a planet beyond Rofus that is orbiting around Vega. It must therefore have been the tenth planet. They were at the beginning of their space era and this was one of their first bigger expeditions. Our ancestors understood very little of technical things but sensed that what was happening would at some future date be of great importance and so they made reports that have survived to

77

this day. Hence our exact knowledge of these events.'

The thought crossed Rhodan's mind that the Thort had pretended they knew hardly anything at all today of the events of that time. He must therefore have changed his opinion.

Ishy reported that Lossoshér was still speaking the truth.

'The leader of the expedition made a gift of the strange instruments to the Thort and also gave him the exact construction plans, which our leader at that time placed in the Red Palace under the precautionary security measures of which I previously told you. Then the strangers from space disappeared and all that remained was the memory and the transmitters.'

The scientist fell silent. Rhodan waited, but when nothing further was volunteered he said: 'What do you know today about those strangers that live on the tenth planet? If I'm not mistaken, you can fly there any time you wish. I can't remember your ever mentioning that this planet's inhabited.'

'It's not inhabited, indeed, and according to our explorers, there never has been any life on the tenth planet. It seems the strangers weren't telling us the truth there.'

That was a startling revelation, and Rhodan didn't conceal his disappointment. 'Then you're not sure at all that they originated from this system? Very regrettable. I was most eager to meet the builders of these matter transmitters in person. Too bad. Aren't there any clues where they really came from? What did they look like?'

'Our historial accounts tell nothing about that. Obviously, they must've resembled us or you. And hints . . .' Lossoshér hesitated for a moment.

He's deliberating if he's permitted to tell you about this, signaled the Japanese girl.

Rhodan and Bell were waiting.

'Well, there is someone, but I'm not sure that he'll want

to help you in this matter. During all these years that the aliens had to stay here on our planet, much against their will, not a single one of them died, though there were many among them that looked quite old. When our forefathers wondered about this mysterious longevity, they simply explained, "to be able to live longer than the sun." '

'We have something to go on there.' Rhodan nodded, satisfied. 'We can judge from that, if nothing else, that they could live to a ripe old age. I wonder, though, why they never visited Ferrol again. They certainly had plenty of opportunity during these thousands of years.'

'I quite agree with you there,' replied Lossoshér. 'I've often wondered about that, but I've never been able to figure it out. There seems to be no logical explanation. Just two possibilities might be considered: either the strangers originated from another system and never returned to the Vega sector, or their race fell victim to some catastrophe. There's a slight clue in our legends. The leader of the expedition is supposed to have said once to our Thort: "We live longer than the sun, but the sun itself wants to prevent us from doing so." I don't know how to interpret this remark.'

Bell was about to say something, but he caught Rhodan's warning glance just in time. Bell remained silent.

Lossoshér believes that the strangers emigrated from the tenth planet, came Ishy's mute message.

Rhodan beamed a thought in her direction: *In that case, the explorers should have found remnants of their civilization on the tenth planet, Ishy.*

What a puzzling story! Highly developed living beings had existed at some time on the tenth planet and yet not the slightest trace had remained behind. That was most unlikely, for even the smallest nations will leave traces of their presence that can be detected as much as fifty thousand years later. And these aliens – apparently immortals, capable of space travel and five-dimensional thought processes – no, it was impossible that they should've vanished without any trace. . . .

But where had they gone to? Where were they now?

Rhodan rose quickly. 'I'm very grateful, Lossoshér, for your valuable hints. I know you're just as interested as I to find an answer to all these problems. Therefore I suggest that as soon as we've chased the Topides from this world, you accompany me on a trip to the tenth planet. Both of us together might find some further clues, let's hope.'

'It'll be a great honor for me,' the scientist assured him, shaking Rhodan's outstretched hand. 'An old dream might come true for me this way.' He shook hands with Ishy and Bell, and continued: 'According to our exploratory flights to the tenth planet, you shouldn't encounter any difficulties either, particularly since your ships fly so much faster than ours. I don't think the gap between Rofus and the tenth planet will present any special problems there.'

For a moment Rhodan stood there, startled, but he smiled quickly with an air of assurance.

'Oh, certainly not,' he said, and shoved Bell through the door. 'Most definitely not, Lossoshér. . . .'

Chapter Four

THE GREATEST MYSTERY OF THE UNIVERSE

The Topides were preparing everything for the landing of the special envoy ships due to arrive from the home planet. Meanwhile Perry Rhodan made his first serious attempt to steal the plans for the construction of the matter transmitters. He had to obtain these plans to forestall unpleasant future surprises.

He was accompanied by Tako Kakuta and Ras Tschubai, the teleporters. The secret one-man transmitter transported the three men inside the Red Palace. Wuriu Sengu had made a sketch for them showing the way to the hidden vault. Oddly enough, the Japanese seer had failed to penetrate the walls of the crypt with his eyes. He couldn't see through its walls. For the first time his eyes met an obstacle that couldn't be changed structurally and thus become transparent for his special eyesight.

But at least Rhodan knew the location of the crypt.

They had to proceed very cautiously. The palace was bustling with activity. The teleporters executed lightning-fast jumps and first scouted out each path to enable Rhodan to make his way unimpeded by any danger. They mostly used secret passages within the thick walls, but more than once they had to cross corridors and wide halls. This wasn't always without risk.

Finally they reached the lower and less busy zones of the gigantic palace. Then they entered an area that was below the ground.

Tako Kakuta returned from one of his jumps. 'There's a corridor ahead of us that makes a sharp turn and then opens into a large hall. According to Sengu's sketch we should find the vault in the middle of it. I'm afraid you'll get the surprise of your lives.'

Rhodan didn't ask any questions. He followed the Japanese, while the African covered the rear.

There was no door at the end of the corridor. It suddenly widened to a very large room, a hundred and fifty feet by a hundred and fifty. The ceiling was roughly fifteen feet high.

They used their searchlights, trying to pierce the dark vault. But the bright light cones met only dark, bare walls. It took a few seconds for Rhodan to establish that the subterranean room was empty. Puzzled, he examined again Sengu's sketch. Both friends looked over his shoulder.

'That's right – it must be this room. The vault's supposed to be in the middle.' Rhodan looked up from the drawing. 'I can't find it here. Maybe Sengu made a mistake and there's still another hall a bit lower.'

'I'll have a look,' Ras volunteered, and vanished instantaneously. A little while later he reappeared, obviously bewildered. 'No, we're directly above solid rocks here. There are no other empty chambers below this level here. The vault we're looking for can't be above us. That means it must be here. But where? Sengu undeniably saw the vault, therefore it cannot have become invisible all of a sudden. After all, it was the only thing that Sengu failed to make invisible, because he couldn't penetrate it with his eyes. That would be a paradox.'

'Maybe,' Rhodan began to ponder aloud, staring at the opposite wall. 'Maybe just what appears to be a paradox happens to be the truth when you think in a five-dimensional manner.'

'What do you mean by that?'

'Our seer Sengu is capable of altering the atomic structure of matter in such a way that it becomes transparent for his eyes. With the exception of the vault, which is surrounded by a five-dimensional screen. It remained visible to his eyes. Therefore it must be right here, beyond a doubt. But we can't perceive it. That means, for us, who aren't seers like our friend Sengu, it remains invisible. I bet if Sengu were here with us, standing where I am now, and using his "normal" eyesight, he couldn't see anything either.'

'I don't understand that,' admitted Ras Tschubai.

'To be frank with you I can't understand it either too well.' Rhodan smiled. 'Let's walk over to the spot where the vault's supposed to be.'

They advanced a few steps and then ran into the invisible obstacle. Rhodan, who'd walked slowly, hands held out in front of him, didn't seem to be surprised. He just chuckled to himself, as if he hadn't expected anything different.

'I thought so! A mirror effect that's turned into solid matter. A solidified vision. That's great – but incomprehensible.'

Tako gently stroked the smooth surface of the 'nothingness.' 'But there's nothing to be seen. Just like air. . . .'

'Sengu's eyes couldn't penetrate this "nothingness" and neither can our eyes. We just imagine we can do it, that's all. The mirror effect changes from every visual angle we try to look at it, and that gives the impression that we can see the opposite side of the room. Ras, walk over to the other side of the room, please, then tell me whether you can see us or not. But be sure to steer clear of the vault; make a wide circle around it.'

The black man walked along the wall and stopped when he arrived at a spot directly opposite Rhodan and Tako.

Between them was the invisible 'nothingness'. They couldn't see each other.

'In spite of all,' said Rhodan, 'it isn't transparent, even for Sengu. Only – if Sengu cannot penetrate it with his eyes, you won't be able to do it either. Tako, you won't manage to penetrate it, even when you dematerialize. Why don't you try it?'

Tako didn't lose a second. The place in which he'd just been standing was empty now. Rhodan had wanted to add something more, but the Japanese had acted too quickly. A wild shriek of pain echoed loudly in the stillness of the giant chamber. Rhodan and Ras were startled out of their wits. Then they observed an odd spectacle.

Tako materialized in mid-air. He slid downward along the invisible wall, arms and legs spread apart, desperately seeking to hold onto something. His face was a horrified question mark. He landed on his feet, standing once more on solid ground, looking perplexed, trembling all over.

'What in the world was that?' he cried out.

'The barrier,' explained Perry Rhodan. 'While you were dematerialized, trying to fly inside the vault, you bumped into the barrier surrounding it. You materialized again and simply skidded down along its side. That's all. You see, you can't penetrate the screen either. I hope the robot brain will be able to give us an answer to that – I can't find it by myself.'

Ras walked gingerly along the wall, rejoining his two friends.

'That's weird,' he said. 'Is that an energy screen?'

'I don't think so Ras. A teleporter can get through an energy screen quite easily, but never through a five-dimensional field. The field doesn't exist here where we are; it's somewhere else. I can't quite explain this; I'm sort of guessing. I can't find the proper words. I might be standing at the threshold of comprehending this strange phenomenon. I've some vague idea how all this is interrelated, just enough to supply the necessary data to the electronic brain in our *Stardust II*. Perhaps the brain will be able to find the answer to this mystery. Let's leave; no use wasting our time here any longer.'

In silence the three men started on their way back.

The empty hall remained behind, and inside, the greatest mystery of the universe.

Bell's hour of triumph had arrived. Bright and early in the morning he assembled his mutants, showing off in the worst possible way. He was telling all kinds of crazy jokes, which so exasperated Anne Sloane that she had him float up to the roof of a Sicha house. But this didn't disturb Reg Bell. He simply continued his tale how, once upon a time long ago, he'd cut off the buttons from his sergeant's pants, and then had sewed them back on again, but all in the wrong places. He described these spots in all detail, which again drove Anne to lift him off the roof, leaving him suspended in mid-air.

'If you don't stop, Reg, I'll let go, and let you drop to the ground, all two hundred pounds of you!' threatened Anne.

Bell was waving his arms and legs, jerking around helplessly.

'I've heard worse threats from my sergeant, but never such insults. Two hundred pounds! How dare you, Anne. You know I only weigh . . .'

'*Mister* Bell!' It was John Marshall, the telepath. 'Your jokes aren't as funny as you might think. Tell us the stories about your sergeant's pants when we men are alone! Anne's quite right to let you dangle up there.'

'That doesn't bother me,' protested Bell, but his voice

quavered a bit. 'I'm only fifteen feet above ground. . . .'

'Don't forget, gravity's greater here than back home. You can break every single bone in your body if I let go,' warned Anne. 'Be reasonable, then I'll let you come down safely.'

'I'll come down by myself,' said Bell, and tried to reach for the edge of the roof. But it was too far away. 'Tama Yokida, come and get me! We men must stick together!'

The slender Japanese, a telekinetic like Anne Sloane, took over. He let Bell drift closer to the roof. Bell grasped the rain gutter and climbed onto the wooden shingles.

'Bring a ladder!' he ordered. 'We men must demonstrate that we don't depend on women!' He overlooked the fact that the ladder sailed through the air as if pushed by invisible ghosts, then leaned against the side of the house. He climbed down slowly, planting himself in front of the pretty young girl. 'I must express my disapproval, young lady. You're abusing your precious talents.'

'You're right.' Anne laughed. 'I've been using them on worthless objects.'

Everyone joined in the laughter, although nobody – except for the telepaths – knew whether her remark had referred to Bell or the ladder.

Their fun was suddenly interrupted by a message coming from the sender of the resistance groups. The Topidian envoy ship had entered the system and was approaching Ferrol. The time for action had come for Bell and his mutant corps.

Bell's mood changed abruptly. Now he was serious and matter-of-fact. 'Wuriu Sengu is to go first. Anne Sloane will follow him as the telekinetic and then André Noir as the hypno. The others will stand by. They'll follow as soon as I send further instructions. Is that clear?'

He didn't wait for their answer, but stepped into the small

wire cage and disappeared almost at once. The mutants
followed in the order Bell had indicated.

More than two hundred rod-shaped Topidian cruisers,
with their characteristic bulge around the middle, were lined
up in closed ranks at the giant spaceport of Thorta. Their
crews were standing at attention in front of their battleships,
ready for a final inspection by Trker-Hon, who had been
named commander of the Topidian fleet. Shortly afterward,
Trker-Hon returned to the Red Palace. Rok-Gor was
already waiting for him.

'Everything's ready for the arrival of the commissioner,'
announced Trker-Hon. 'When's his ship supposed to land?'

'Any moment now.' Rok hesitated slightly before he inquired: 'Have there been any further – incidents?'

'None; everything's normal again. Maybe the Ferrons
have given up all this nonsense.'

'Not the Ferrons,' Rok corrected in an irritated voice,
'the Arkonides! As soon as the commissioner leaves after
his investigation, and if all goes smoothly, we're going to
annihilate the ninth planet. We must teach these impertinent
imperialists a lesson. Where's Chrekt-Orn?'

'He's waiting at the spaceport.'

'All right then, let's go!'

Everything had been prepared in the best manner, according to Topidian standards. A platform had been erected
directly in front of the crews, and TV cameras and hyper-
transmitters had been set up. Rok-Gor was very eager that
the Despot – over eight hundred light-years away – should
witness his hour of glory. He wanted to convince the ruler
how excellent his decision had been to have nominated him,
Rok-Gor, as the commander-in-chief of the expeditionary
forces. It would be only a question of time now until he'd
be promoted to the position of space admiral. That this pro-

motion would mean exile or even death for the unfortunate Chrekt-Orn didn't bother him in the least.

It wasn't surprising, therefore, that Chrekt-Orn was awaiting the commissioner's arrival with very mixed emotions. André Noir, who 'listened in' to Chrekt's thoughts for a while, even felt a little sorry for him. He decided that he needed to be taught a lesson which he wouldn't forget for some time.

The car stopped. The commander-in-chief and Trker-Hon got out. Rok-Gor used the remaining time for an inspection of the troops. The war had apparently been forgotten; they acted as if no hostilities had ever existed, while ultrafast scout ships patrolled the space around Ferrol, making sure no unpleasant suprises would disturb the commissioner's visit. The Topides, at least, believed these precautionary measures would do the trick.

Meanwhile, hidden in the secret chamber, Bell had Sengu give a nonstop report on the events at the spaceport. The seer could watch the scene as if he were present in person.

'He's about to finish inspecting the troops – what a pompous ass, this new commander! He did nothing to deserve this promotion. He got his post only because we let Chrekt-Orn swing from the chandelier. . . . The special envoy craft's arriving. What a huge crate – by Topidian standards, of course. It's one of those cigar-shaped ships with a bulging middle. It's landing now. The troops are presenting arms. The entrance hatch is opening. A lizard-man's coming out. Wow, what a uniform! I've never seen anything as colorful as that. André, it's your turn now. I can't hear what's being said. You can read their thoughts.'

And André Noir went to work.

The commissioner and his entourage had stepped onto the platform directly from the ship. The commissioner walked ahead while his men, about twenty Topide officers, kept at a respectful distance to show the honor that was due him. Inside the vessel, the hyper-transmitters were busy sending an instantaneous account of what was happening here. This way the ruler on Topid became an eyewitness to the galactic event.

Rok-Gor marched stiffly toward the commissioner, who was waiting for him to come close. Rok-Gor saluted. 'Welcome to the Despot's envoy on the conquered eighth planet of the Vega system. The situation here on Ferrol is calm, our forces are superior and the final defeat of the enemy is at hand.'

The commissioner came immediately to the point. 'How about the inexcusable blunder we've heard about? Chrekt-Orn, what have you to say in your defense?'

The former commander-in-chief had kept humbly in the background. He stepped to the fore now, conscience-stricken. His black lizard eyes looked sad and frightened. 'We're fighting not only against the local Ferrons,' he said, 'but also against the hated Arkonides. They've already established themselves in this part of the universe, as could be expected after having intercepted the distress signal. Their superior fighting forces and weapons . . .'

'Superior?' shouted the commissioner, and threw a questioning glance at Rok-Gor. 'I was just told that this campaign has practically been won.'

André Noir took over the helpless Chrekt-Orn. 'It has hardly begun,' Chrekt croaked firmly. 'Rok-Gor hides from you all the difficulties which he can't handle. Topides have come under magic spells, lifeless objects begin floating and flying through the air, our commanders are losing control over their battleships, they start shooting at our own cruisers, our officers seem to be losing their minds, they are totally confused. . . .'

'Lies, nothing but lies!' Rok-Gor yelled, full of fury.

'Chrekt-Orn wants to cover up for his own inefficiency. We're not dealing with any supernatural enemy forces!'

'True, the opponents are quite normal beings, nothing supernatural about them. They're simply superior to us. In my humble opinion, it would be advisable to leave this system at once.'

The commissioner listened attentively. He felt alarmed at this war of words. 'Why all these different explanations? What's really been going on here?'

'A great deal!' Chrekt cried out. 'Mutiny among the officers. . . .'

'They were properly punished!' Rok-Gor interrupted. 'These things will happen occasionally. And there's no reason why we should break off our victorious campaign.'

'The Arkonides have come to the aid of the Ferrons, Commissioner. They have new weapons that can take over the minds of other creatures. They can even seize control of our cruisers this way.'

A voice came over the loudspeakers of the Topide envoy ship. 'This is the Despot speaking! I demand an immediate explanation of what's happened on Ferrol! Whoever the enemy may be, he must be defeated. And if Rok-Gor isn't capable of doing so, I'll simply have to replace him with a better man. Where's Trker-Hon?'

'Down with the Despot!' shouted the new commander of the Topidian battle fleet. 'Down with his commissioner!'

'What did you say?' screamed the outraged commissioner. He cocked his head to one side, trying to understand. He couldn't believe his ears. Trker-Hon came closer.

'You heard me right the first time! I said, down with the tyranny of the Despot. We have no business being here. The Ferrons haven't done any harm to us. Down with the commissioner! We don't need any spies and informers here!'

The tall lizard on the platform was gasping for air. He signaled with his left clawed hand. Rayguns flashed as his companions drew their arms lightning fast from their holsters.

'Mutiny! We have a mutiny on our hands, Despot!' the commissioner announced. 'What are your orders?'

'Death for all mutineers!' commanded the Despot from over eight hundred light-years away.

Rok-Gor suddenly drew his raygun. He pointed it at the commissioner and pulled the trigger. The highest dignitary of the Despot died instantly. His companions froze in horror, but a moment later they opened fire and killed Rok-Gor on the spot. Then they withdrew hastily to the safety of their ship.

Once more the Despot's voice came over the loud-speakers. 'Chrekt-Orn, report back to Topid as soon as you've brought the campaign to a glorious end. And if you should send me a message of defeat of our own forces, this will seal your death warrant. In case you should try to avoid just punishment and fail to return to Topid, you can rest assured that my men will find you. They'll pursue you to the farthest corners of the universe. You as well as your officers.'

The voice over the loudspeaker broke off. The big ship trembled, and lifted off. It raced up into the skies with un-believable speed, and soon disappeared from view. A few seconds later a deadly silence covered the spaceport. Then suddenly, Trker-Hon began to shout at the top of his voice: 'Long live our Despot! Long live our glorious Despot! May he reign forever!'

Cruiser Number Thirty-seven rose gently from the ground, ascended vertically, looped the loop and peppered the parade ground with a broadside of neutron beams. The lizards fell to the ground, seeking cover. Trker-Hon yelled hysterical commands, ordering an officer to take up a fighter plane, pursue the cruiser and arrest its crew. He was horrified to discover that the cruiser had started without any men on board.

Trker-Hon realized that his entire fleet might take off any moment the same as Cruiser Number Thirty-seven had done. He knew now that the Ferrons had become invincible with the aid of the Arkonides.

'All men aboard! Into the cruisers!' he screamed, terrified. 'We're leaving Ferrol this instant! Stand by for further instructions!'

Back in the secret chamber of the Red Palace, André Noir listened to Trker-Hon's final commands with satisfaction.

'That's his own decision,' he said to Bell. 'I didn't suggest this order to him. I hope they've finally come to their senses. And as Sengu can see, Chrekt-Orn doesn't put up any opposition to these commands. On the contrary. He's in favor of instant flight. I think we've gotten rid of those lizards. Anne, how about a final demonstration?'

The young girl seized Sengu's arm. 'I'll have a look at the scene out there,' she said. Bell was seized by a feverish fighting mood. What wouldn't he have given to be right on the scene! But worse still, he couldn't 'see' like the mutants what was going on. But then he remembered: the Red Palace must be free now of enemy forces. He could simply take the elevator and ride up to the roof and observe everything from up there with his own eyes.

'Wait a couple of minutes, Anne, then have the lizards execute some fine military drills high up in the air!' Bell stormed out of the secret chamber and raced along the corridors. His friends could hear his hurried steps grow more and more distant.

'He's a daredevil, taking unnecessary risks,' growled

André. Then he concentrated again on his mental observations. 'What's happening now, Sengu?'

'Orderly retreat,' replied the Japanese. 'Seems, though, that they're leaving most of their equipment in Thorta. Maybe they'll want to pick it up later on.'

'I'll cure them of that notion right away,' promised Anne. She waited for two minutes, then Sengu reported that Bell had made his way safely up to the roof and was standing there looking over to the spaceport. Only then did the young girl start to concentrate with an intensity she had never achieved before.

'I think the lizards will never return to Ferrol to get the rest of their equipment,' said Perry Rhodan to the Thort. 'Bell and his mutant corps have taught them a fine lesson and frightened them out of their wits. They won't ever forget that, I'm sure. I wouldn't be surprised if they'd leave the Vega sector for good.'

Thora, who'd taken part in the conversation, as well as Khrest, shook her head. 'The electronic brain's predicted with a probability of ninety-nine percent that the Topides will *not* leave this system. You know what fate awaits them on Topid. Chrekt-Orn and Trker-Hon will search for some uninhabited planet and settle there rather than face their Despot. The brain's assumptions agree with our own first-hand experiences in our dealings with the lizard race. It behooves us not to let them out of our sight.'

Bell, who'd just arrived from Thorta, shrugged his shoulders.

'They've had it for good. You should've seen how our little Anne had the fleet dance in the air, all in rhythm. What a sight; the flagship was waltzing around with a patrol cruiser.'

93

'They prefer ghosts to death,' replied Thora. 'Especially if the ghosts like to fool around.'

'I gave them a good run for their money!' Bell protested. 'I wasn't too soft on them.'

'We must admit that you've victoriously brought an end to an interplanetary conflict, which really should be called an interstellar one, with a minimal loss of life. Rok-Gor and the commissioner paid with their lives, and one ship was lost. You were very merciful indeed!'

'I was the one who ordered Bell to use these tactics,' Rhodan defended his friend. 'Deringhouse and his squadron fighters are following the fleeing enemy to observe their movements. I expect to hear from him at any moment. According to his latest report the three hundred seventy Topidian vessels have already crossed the orbit of the thirty-eighth planet.'

'They seem to be fleeing, indeed,' Thora expressed her bewilderment. 'Could the electronic brain be so wrong about that?'

Rhodan didn't answer. He didn't believe either that the electronic brain might be making a mistake. What was it, then, that the Topides were planning, knowing full well that they didn't have a . . . ghost . . . of a chance in this sector of the universe?

Chapter Five

THE INFINITY BOX

Forty-two planets were revolving around the bluish Vega sun. The outermost planets were ice worlds, totally devoid of life. The sun was too distant for its warming rays to have reached the lonely wanderers.

One of the disadvantaged members of the Vegan solar system, the fortieth planet, was circled by six moons that showed no phases and remained forever dark. These moons were the size of small to medium planets in reality. They weren't different in any respect from the huge world whose gravitational pull made them its constantly swirling prisoners.

The fortieth planet was a gigantic world. No wonder that it formed its own system together with its six moons, the smallest being about the size of Pluto. One of these six moons even possessed a satellite of its own, as large as a continent – a cosmic curiosity.

Deringhouse and his space-fighter squadron were in hot pursuit of the fleeing Topidian fleet, which was just crossing the orbit of the thirty-ninth planet. To Deringhouse's great surprise, the enemy suddenly deviated from its straight course and entered the orbital path of the fortieth planet. He'd assumed the enemy would head out of the system and then vanish into hyperspace. And now this!

But this wasn't the only surprise the Topidian fleet had in store for him. The cigar-shaped ships with the bulging middles broke rank, forming six equal-sized groups, and dispersed, each in a different direction. Deringhouse had the presence of mind to send some of his fighters after each of the lizards' smaller formations. He kept in constant touch with his men via long-range videophone. Because of this he had a pretty good idea what was happening.

The Topides had no intention whatsoever of abandoning their plans regarding the Vega system. Return to their home planet was out of the question, unless they came as victors. Therefore they hit upon the obvious solution: withdrawal to the outermost reaches of the Vega system, where they'd try to establish a new strong hold. The six moons of the fortieth planet seemed the ideal spot for this.

Deringhouse gave orders to six of his fighter planes to stay behind and keep the Topidian fleet under constant surveillance. They were to inform him of any suspicious moves of the enemy. Then Deringhouse, accompanied by the rest of his squadron, set course again for Rofus in order to give a personal report to Perry Rhodan about the unexpected turn of events.

To his great dismay, his news didn't result in the startled reaction he'd imagined. Rhodan listened calmly and then issued orders to ring the fortieth planet with patrol posts, at the proper distance, of course, to make sure that the lizards wouldn't suddenly start out on a surprise attack on the inner planets of the Vega system. Then he added:

'There are several more important things I want to see taken care of. You'll be in charge of the guard detail, Deringhouse, that will send out the alarm in case the lizards try to start new trouble. Thanks, that's all.' Rhodan waited until Deringhouse had left. Then he turned to Bell, who'd watched the scene, sitting quietly in a chair. 'Go and get the Thort, Reg! Also Khrest and Thora. I want to have a talk with them.'

'May I stay here during this meeting?'

'Absolutely. You have to be here with us, Reg. Also, get

96

John Marshall to come here. I want to make sure that the Thort isn't trying to pull the wool over my eyes. He's been known to have lied before. . . . Now, get a move on, friend!'

'Your wish is my command, sir,' mocked Bell. 'I'll be back in no time.' He got out of his chair as slowly as he possibly could, and dragged his feet, then left the room with a nonchalant grin.

Rhodan didn't pay any attention to his antics, he was already lost in thoughts: *The Topides are just a secondary problem that will find its solution in due time. The more immediate problem is the Ferrons. And especially the Thort. We've helped them out of a critical situation, and they owe us a debt of gratitude. But they don't seem too much inclined to be grateful, and willing to do us some favors in return now. I'll simply have to force them to do so. The secret of the matter transmitters . . .*

Khrest and Thora were the first to arrive. The sage old Arkonide scientist shook hands with Rhodan and took a seat next to him. Thora, apparently in a more affable mood than usual, smiled and held Rhodan's hand for a second longer than was really necessary. There was something in her eyes that caused Rhodan to wonder; he was filled with rather pleasant emotions at this unexpected change in her. He knew he could count on her support, for today at least – and this was unfortunately so rarely the case.

'I'm glad you got here before the Thort,' Rhodan began. 'I'd like to inform you about my plans. I know you're as much interested in the transmitter as I am myself. We must obtain the designs and blueprints for its construction, at all costs. The Thort isn't going to supply them to us voluntarily, even if he had them in his possession. But I'm sure he can give us at least some hints as to how we can get them. Lossoshér revealed that there's some kind of a formula, known only to the Thort. This secret formula has been handed down through generations from Thort to Thort. Too bad they have no idea what to do with it. I believe this formula is the encoded password that will open the five-dimensional lock of the secret vault.'

'Do you really think the Ferron will disclose this formula to you?' Thora asked.

'He'll have to.' Rhodan smiled. 'If he won't hand it over willingly, then we'll find other means to make him part with it. After all, that's a job for the mutant corps. Somebody will take over his mind and . . .'

Now Bell entered together with the Thort. John Marshall followed on their heels. They nodded a silent greeting and sat down. The Thort appeared to be in low spirits; he certainly guessed what was awaiting him.

Perry Rhodan came quickly to the point.

'The Topides have been chased away from Ferrol; nothing stands in the way any longer for the Ferronian government to return to their homeland. The time has come, therefore, Thort, for us to say goodbye.'

The leader of the Ferrons could hardly hide his fear. 'But the Topides are still somewhere within our solar system,' he objected timidly. 'I've just learned this from your friend Bell. You know very well that we're incapable of warding off a renewed invasion all by ourselves.'

Rhodan leaned forward, closer to the Thort.

'I wonder why I even bothered coming to your assistance, Thort.' Rhodan spoke with great insistence. 'But you make no attempt to help us in return. True, I'll admit, you allowed the scientist Lossoshér to reveal some of the background on how you came into possession of the matter transmitters. But what good does this knowledge do us? The few machines of this amazing invention are in your hands. I must get the construction plans; I must know how more of these wonderful machines can be built by us. Those blueprints that you gave me some time ago were nothing but skillful forgeries. You tried to put me off with these worthless plans. You realize, of course, that five-dimensional thought processes are impossible to express in three-dimensional figures. You have a choice now: if you wish to enjoy our protection in the future, if you want to make sure that your realm will survive, then you must tell us how to open the crypt in the Red Palace. Otherwise we'll leave you here to your own devices and to certain defeat at the hands of the lizard invaders.'

Rhodan had put his cards on the table. The Thort knew exactly what was wanted of him. He had to come to a decision. Marshall signaled that the Ferronian leader wasn't thinking of treason. He was toying with the thought of coming out with the truth. But it took several minutes until he could definitely make up his mind.

'I know of some clue, but I doubt it will bring you closer to the solution of your problem. I'd like to know something first, though: what will happen once you can construct these matter transmitters?'

Khrest took it upon himself to answer. 'I don't understand your concern in this matter, Thort. Are you afraid, maybe, that this would change the course of history in our universe? We possess space ships that work on the same basic principle as your matter transmitters. We dematerialize and continue our journey in hyperspace. This is what happens in your matter transmitters, too. We're only interested in a simplification of this method, that's all. I assure you, our galaxy won't go to rack and ruin, if this is what you're afraid of, Thort.'

'But the wise ones that entrusted this secret to us were thinking ahead. They considered it essential that only those persons would comprehend the method of construction who had acquired the necessary maturity – even if this would take millions of years. Why should we break this law now?'

Rhodan advanced the decisive argument. 'You give us the secret formula, and if we succeed in opening the vault, this would be sufficient proof of our degree of maturity, don't you agree?'

The Thort looked into Rhodan's questioning eyes. For a moment he seemed to be overwhelmed by Rhodan's compelling glance, to be swallowed up by this ocean of steely strength. Then, mustering all his forces of resistance, he freed himself from this almost hypnotic compulsion, and arrived at a decision out of his own free will.

'I see your point.' He conceded defeat. 'I'll hand this formula over to you. It's very simple and easy to remember – but it doesn't make any sense to me. This is it: *Dimension X = pentagon of space-time simultan.* That's all.'

All were silent.

Khrest and Thora exchanged quick glances, which plainly showed they neither understood the formula nor had come to some concensus of opinion. Bell opened his mouth wide as if to yawn, but then seemed to reconsider, and closed his mouth, sighing noisily.

John Marshall signaled silently: *That's all, indeed.*

Rhodan concentrated on memorizing the mysterious words of the formula.

Breaking the general silence, the Thort remarked, not without a trace of gratification: 'I'm sorry that you obviously don't know what to make of these words either. We've known this formula for thousands of years, but its meaning has remained a mystery to us to this day. I've done all now that's within my power, and I hope that you'll appreciate my effort.'

Rhodan nodded casually. 'Thank you, Thort. We certainly appreciate this. But let's discuss something now of more immediate importance, the real reason why I've called this meeting. When do you intend to return to Ferrol, Thort?'

The Thort reacted to this change of topic with obvious relief.

'We've already begun with our preparations. Our fleet's ready to start. I and some of the members of my government will return this very day to Ferrol via matter transmitter. We'll proceed directly to Thorta; the receiving stations have been set up there in the meantime. There'll be a big victory celebration and I'd like to invite both you and your friends to honor us with your presence there.'

'Thanks,' replied Rhodan with a hint of sarcasm. 'We'll certainly accept this invitation. At the same time I'd like to ask you to put at our disposal a restricted area where we'll erect a base for your protection against any alien enemies.'

'Don't you plan on staying here on Rofus?' asked the Thort.

'No. When the Topides renew the battle, they'll attack Ferrol and not Rofus. Besides, I have other reasons.'

It was easy to see that the Thort would have loved knowing these reasons, but he didn't dare ask what they were. He simply said: 'We'll decide about that after our victory celebration. I hardly believe that there'll be any objections to your request. Since our business has been concluded I'd like to ask your permission to leave now. My people . . .'

He had barely left the room when Bell gave vent to his pent-up feelings. He breathed deeply, then exhaled forcefully and noisily, as if he were afraid that he might otherwise burst.

'How about that formula?' he exploded impatiently. His eyes were aglitter with curiosity. Khrest and Thora glanced at Rhodan who, evidently bored by all this excitement, studied some invisible speck high up on the ceiling. 'Why do you ask me? How should I know?'

Khrest's face showed something akin to disappointment, while Thora smiled disdainfully.

'Who else, Perry? Who else could I ask?' Bell insisted.

'The same authority I'm going to consult for advice now,' Rhodan answered, and started to leave the room.

He'd almost reached the door, but Bell had rushed over to him and grasped his arm. 'And who would that be, Perry?'

'The positronic super brain on the *Stardust II*, of course, my friend.'

Now Khrest's face also lit up with a smile. But his smile held no sarcasm, only pleasure.

The first big victory party had come and gone and the second even bigger one was supposed to follow shortly.

The Thort had taken up residence again in the Red Palace and had resumed his official duties. All signs of the invaders' occupation were quickly removed everywhere on Ferrol. The population was overjoyed to return to their normal daily lives.

Rhodan's request for a base was granted without delay by the hastily called assembly of the ministers' council. The restricted area was situated near the mountains, which were the home of the Sichas. The following day, the *Stardust II* landed in the rocky desert. The ship's powerful ray beams created an immense cave, more than one thousand yards deep. Quickly the giant spacesphere hid inside, disappearing from the surface of the eighth planet. Labor robots soon set to work and constructed Rhodan's first galactic base. Corridors, elevators living quarters, workshops and laboratories were built. Storerooms and hangars for the space-fighters were installed in the molten rock. Finally, an Arkonide reactor supplied the power to erect an enormous energy screen above the whole installation, rendering it thus unassailable.

The native population watched all this activity with mixed emotions, as Rhodan's mutant corps easily found out. The Ferrons were none too happy to see the former occupational enemy forces being replaced by some new type of regimentation. Rhodan kept reassuring the Thort that his people would only derive benefit from this military base. But how could the Ferrons comprehend what Rhodan meant by that? How could they know that Rhodan considered them to be the first colony of the galactic empire he intended to create?

In addition to all the planning and work that went into the establishment of his first galactic base, Rhodan's mind was set upon solving the problem that was his foremost concern. He made his final preparations to wrest the big mystery from the dim past of Ferronian history. He held a lengthy dialogue with the gigantic brain in the *Stardust II*, presenting to it the formula he'd obtained from the Thort. Rhodan learned the answers he'd hoped for. At this juncture Khrest joined him in the huge room which housed the positronic brain.

'I knew you'd choose the only possible way, the right way,' Khrest commented.

'Was there any other way, Khrest? The positronic brain is thinking in a five-dimensional manner – the same way you do and I myself, at least partially thanks to my hypnopsych training. However, neither you nor I could've found the solution on our own, as simple as it appears to be. The whole secret is contained in this notion of "simultan". Also "pentagon" plays a role. But only everything in its proper combination, in its overall "gestalt", makes sense.'

'Doesn't five-dimensional thought always make sense?' Khrest smiled gently.

'Not in our universe,' replied Rhodan, and he smiled, too. 'But to be frank with you, Khrest, I'm a bit disappointed. The five-dimensionally secured vault is in reality a quite normal four-dimensional affair. The documents do exist, but not in the present time – that is the fourth-dimensional factor of the mystery. The protective shield consists of transformed radiowaves of far distant radio stars – well, simply cosmic rays. Add to that some technical tricks, effects created by bending light rays, and naturally existing energy walls. All these obstacles can be rendered ineffective when certain events occur at the "simultan" instant.'

'And how do you intend to cause these events to occur?' Khrest asked with a certain curiosity that revealed unmistakably that he already knew the answer. Rhodan played along with him.

'I'll use my mutants. Tanaka Seiko is a natural-born detection finder. He can receive normal radiowaves, sent by intelligent living beings and understand them. But in addition to that, he can also receive the waves emanating from the radio stars – the same waves that form the energy screen around the secret vault. If he succeeds in deflecting them, we'll gain unhindered access to the documents, which will simultaneously be brought to the present time. That, in a nutshell, is the whole problem.'

'Do you have any idea why and how all this comes about?'

'No, Khrest, I must confess that I really don't know. I told you all the information that the positronic brain supplied to me. Tanaka won't be able to manage by himself, but together with several other mutants it will be possible, thanks to the fact that their individual gifts can be combined in their effect when the mutants touch each other or hold hands. I'll need a telekinetic and a teleporter and, of course, also Sengu, who will announce when the barrier collapses.'

'What will become of these plans?' Thora had entered the room, unnoticed by the two men, who turned around on hearing her question. Thora looked inquiringly at Rhodan with her unfathomable red-gold eyes.

Khrest tried to act as a mediator. 'In case Rhodan should obtain them, he has a claim on them, for otherwise he'd never succeed in opening the vault.'

'He does that with the help of the Arkonide brain.'

'Which would no longer exist if it hadn't been for his intervention at the time – at least not as far as we're concerned. Therefore . . .'

'A very logical argument, indeed,' Thora scoffed, unconvinced but in a more conciliatory mood. 'What will Rhodan do with these plans?'

Khrest shrugged his shoulders. 'That's his affair. Why should he not build any transmitters? Perhaps we might even establish a direct connection between Terra and Arkon. Who knows what potential developments the future might bring?'

Rhodan decided the moment had come for him to enter into the argument. He tried to reassure Thora. 'Thora, don't worry. I'd never build the transmitter unless all of us agreed on it. The secret will belong to all of us. Please – trust me!'

It was the first time in quite a while that he spoke to her in such a personal manner, but she didn't seem to notice. She pretended to have forgotten the brief period in the past when she and Rhodan had come closer to each other. Once again he'd become for her the ambitious Terran who threatened to topple over with one mighty sweep the tottering interstellar empire of the Arkonides.

'I thought it necessary to express my doubts, if you don't mind, Rhodan. But if Khrest agrees with you – well, I won't oppose him. But I have warned you, Khrest!'

She didn't wait for an answer but left the room.

Khrest looked at the control board of the positronic brain. 'We could consult it,' he suggested. Rhodan shook his head. 'Consult it to find out whether I'm reliable or not? No thanks. In case you have your doubts too, Khrest, you can ask the brain when I'm not in the room. After all, I wouldn't want anyone to say that the brain was under undue influence.'

There was a bitter smile around Rhodan's mouth as he turned to leave the room.

Khrest's eyes followed him. There was no expression in them.

The subterranean room was sparsely lit.

Next to Rhodan were standing Bell, Tanaka Seiko, Anne Sloane, Ras Tschubai and Ishy Matsu, the telepath who was endowed with another amazing talent. She had telescopic eyesight. If she concentrated on any place, no matter how far away, she could plainly 'see' what was going on there. Rhodan hoped to make good use of her special talent during the forthcoming experiment.

The Japanese, Tako Kakuta, announced after a few seconds, 'Yes, I can feel it. The cosmic rays that exist everywhere are being bunched together and concentrated right here in this hall. It starts up there near the ceiling. Then the beam expands and forms an opaque cone. I cannot penetrate it at all. Cosmic rays are identical with the passage of time, in my opinion.'

'They do originate from the fourth dimension, after all,' Rhodan whispered almost inaudibly. 'I wonder if you could deflect these waves of the radio stars, or better still, stop them altogether?'

'So that the cone would cease to exist? I'm not sure.'

'You must try it! At the same time, Sengu will concentrate and tell us whether he can see whatever is concealed inside the energy vault.'

Tanaka looked at Anne Sloane. 'If I can let Anne see what I'm seeing, she ought to be able to deflect the rays. They are matter, only in a different form.'

There was apparently nothing in the room in front of them. The invisible vault guarded its secret and wasn't yet ready to yield it.

Tanaka grasped Anne by the arm. The young girl's slender body stiffened and she closed her eyes. Suddenly Sengu shouted: 'There it is!' He pointed to the center of the empty room whose walls were throwing back the dim echo of his excited voice calling out, 'A box – it's gone again. What was that?'

Rhodan felt the excitement coursing hotly through his veins. For a moment he stood as if paralyzed, then pulled himself together.

'A box?'

Tanaka had let go of Anne's arm. The two mutants could not properly concentrate under such circumstances and thus no longer possessed the necessary mental strength to carry through with their task.

'A small, glittering box. It was floating in the center of the room, up there in the air. I could see it for just a second and then it disappeared.'

'It's working this way,' Rhodan whispered. 'Tanaka and Anne, you must try again, but concentrate longer this time. Ras Tschubai will jump the moment Sengu sees the box again. The whole thing mustn't take more than two seconds. I don't know what might happen if Anne's endurance gives out while Ras is still inside the crypt...'

The African's face turned a sickly gray. Sengu put an arm around Tschubai's shoulders. 'Don't worry; I won't startle her again. I won't say a word. I won't do anything to interrupt her. You just watch me. I'll raise my arm, and then you jump at once.'

Ras nodded his head, but didn't reply. His thoughts were probably busy figuring out where he'd be in case Anne or

Tanaka failed in their combined efforts. Then he said: 'I'm ready.'

Rhodan could feel his body vibrate under the tremendous tension. He took a deep breath and then gave the signal.

At first nothing seemed to have changed, but then Rhodan noticed a slight movement in the middle of the room. The air became visible while still remaining transparent. The air began to vibrate and flow, condensing into pale colored spots that merged and separated. And then Rhodan saw the box.

It appeared from nowhere all of a sudden and it shimmered like pure gold. It hovered unsupported above the floor, surrounded by a radiant glow.

Sengu didn't need to give the prearranged signal. Ras Tschubai jumped, for he could perceive the marvelous phenomenon on his own. He simply vanished and then reappeared next to the box. His hands seized the shimmering object and then . . .

Anne called out and collapsed.

Rhodan whirled around and caught her in his arms.

At the same moment Ras and the box vanished from sight. The room was empty once more.

'What happened?' Rhodan asked, and shook Anne, who lay limp as a rag in his arms. 'Anne, Anne! Come on, Anne! What's the matter?'

She opened her eyes and stammered like a child: 'It was too much for me – too great an effort. . . .'

'You must try again! Right away, Anne! Think of Ras! We mustn't leave him in the lurch. Pull yourself together. Tanaka? Ready?'

Rhodan supported Anne, who closed her eyes once more. A tense expression came over her face and made her look like a stranger. Bell was standing a few steps away, rooted to the spot, and said nothing. He didn't dare make a move.

His eyes were staring, wide open, at the spot where Ras Tschubai had been just a moment earlier.

Then the air began to vibrate again; the colors started to flow and run into each other. Ras Tschubai materialized, the box firmly grasped in his hands. He vanished for an instant – only to stand suddenly next to Rhodan, who gently lowered Anne to the ground. He signaled to Bell to come and take care of the totally exhausted young girl.

Rhodan turned to the African, who held the box out to him. Rhodan took the box and gazed at it in awe before he said: 'We almost didn't make it this time, Ras.'

The teleporter smiled weakly and leaned against the wall near the exit. 'I'd never want to go through that experience again. These were the most horrible minutes I ever lived through in all my life.'

'Minutes?' Rhodan wondered aloud. 'But you were hardly a few seconds inside the vault.'

Ras shook his head. 'Impossible! You and the hall disappeared suddenly from view and then I fell into the void. I kept the box clasped in my arms, but no one was there threatening to take it away from me. On the contrary, I had the impression that the box itself was dragging me throughout eternity. For this was exactly what was happening to me. I was racing, faster than thought, out of the galaxy. A few instants later, the galaxy became a gigantic spiral nebula that grew smaller and smaller until it was just one of the millions and millions of specks of light in the universe. I was falling toward a bright spot that was glowing far away, slowly increasing in size. It resembled a window – looking out into infinity, into eternity – or to hell. I couldn't tell, for suddenly the whole process reversed and I was falling back again in the direction where I had come from. The Milky Way loomed larger and larger again. I sank into it – and then I saw this room again. This is what happened to me. But I have no idea what all of this means. . . .'

Rhodan patted Ras's shoulder, trying to calm down the frightened man. 'Ras, you've gone through an experience that no one has ever witnessed before. You were in an energy vault that was suddenly activated and traveled through time. The box, and you with it, returned to the original place where it had been stored – in the past or in the future – who'll ever know for certain? As soon as Anne deflected the waves of the radio stars once more, that had become visible for her by touching Tanaka, the time lock opened again. You were then able to return to the present time and bring the box with you.'

'Time lock?'

Bell and Ras shot out the question simultaneously.

'Of course. There must be something that made this time travel possible for you, Ras. And this mysterious something is the waves of the radio stars. As long as they're beamed into this room where they form an impenetrable energy barrier, the object that had been locked inside remains in a predetermined time period. The moment this barrier was nullified by deflecting the radio beams, the normal conditions were restored again. That's all very simple.'

'Very simple!' exclaimed Bell, whose face plainly showed how baffled he was by all this. 'I haven't the faintest idea what you're talking about. How about the box, Perry?'

Rhodan pressed it against his body as if he were afraid it might be wrested out of his hands again at any moment by some invisible power.

'It's been removed from the time field. Whether we'll manage to open it, that's something else again. Let's hope that Khrest can help us with it. Anne, how are you feeling now?'

The young girl had meanwhile freed herself from Bell's

helpful arms, and stood up straight, leaning gently against Tanaka.

'I'm all right now. It was just the strain that got me.'

'Very well, then,' Rhodan said. 'We'll return to our base. And something else, friends: keep quiet about all of this! It isn't too desirable that all of Ferrol learns of our success here immediately.'

But his warning words came too late. The Thort entered the hall just as Rhodan finished speaking. The Thort looked magnificent in his brightly colored cape. He approached Rhodan and bowed slightly.

'May I be the first to congratulate you on your success. You succeeded where we failed for many centuries.'

Rhodan smiled. 'You needn't be ashamed because of your failures. After all, the Ferrons didn't have the help of a mutant corps.'

'And neither did they have somebody like Perry Rhodan!' added Bell, full of pride, as if he were speaking of his own son. And with these words he solemnly walked ahead of the rest of the group, leaving the hall with the secret time vault.

'It wasn't too difficult after all,' Rhodan finished his report. He'd assembled his men in the mess hall of the *Stardust II* in order to inform them of the successful conclusion of his efforts. Two days had gone by since they'd managed to open the time vault.

'Certainly, we needed to think in a five-dimensional manner up to a certain point, in order to interpret the formula, but the rest could be arrived at by ordinary four-dimensional thought processes. It was just a time lock, made secure by some forces of nature. I must admit, it would've been a hard nut to crack without our mutants' help. Maybe we never could have managed it. The builders of the transmitters wanted to make sure that their invention would become available only to beings of the highest intelligence, who either were already familiar with this invention or who'd never misuse it. I'm confident that we meet these qualifications.'

'Naturally!' It was Reginald Bell. His self-confident remark was greeted with general amusement, although each of the people presented secretly shared his thoughts.

'Once we had the box in our hands, it wasn't difficult to get it open. Our positronic brain figured out the key to the code according to the engraved instructions on the box. Only a five-dimensionally thinking person could have deciphered the symbols. And so, the mystery surrounding the construction of the matter transmitters has been solved.'

'Can we build them now?' Doctor Haggard asked eagerly.

'Of course, as many as we want to,' Rhodan answered. 'But I don't think the right time for it has come yet. Much later, when the many inhabited planets of the universe have established peaceful relations with each other, the transmitters should be used to replace ordinary spaceships. You push a button – and you have traveled many thousands of light-years. But this is still imagination.'

Bell burst out laughing. 'Perry, not too long ago a trip to Mars was considered sheer science fiction. Just think how far we've come in this short time! And you still speak of utopian fantasy!'

Rhodan seemed amused by his friend's reminder that nothing could ever be considered fantastic seen in the light of their recent experiences. He reached for a small case lying on the table in front of him.

'I have a surprise here for Khrest and Thora.' He opened the briefcase and pulled out several very thin metal plates. 'These metal sheets remained when the positronic brain translated the instructions for the building of the matter transmitters. Whenever I presented one of these seven plates, the brain refused to translate them. It said my brain-wave pattern was different from that of the rulers of the universe for whom these instructions were intended. The rulers of the universe are, of course, according to the positronic brain, the Arkonide race.' Rhodan hesitated, then added with respectful appreciation of their antiquity: 'These must certainly be very ancient records.'

Thora threw Perry a quick glance, a question in her eyes. A shrug of Rhodan's shoulders was her only response. Khrest walked over to Rhodan and accepted the metal plates from his hands. He regarded the cryptic records with a frown. Then he spoke slowly: 'This is a language that existed ten thousand years ago. But it's not a simple text, it's written in coded sentences. I wonder what it might be.'

'Perhaps, at last, a clue,' said Rhodan. 'Perhaps finally even a definite message.'

'About what?'

'About the planet of eternal life, Khrest.'

'Then we shall soon find out,' the scientist said softly. '*My* brainwave pattern is that of the Arkonide race.'

Rhodan's gaze followed the two Arkonides as they left the mess hall to consult the positronic brain. He knew they'd reveal the information to him as soon as they themselves found it out and the right opportunity presented itself. In the meantime there were more urgent problems to deal with.

'Manoli!'

The former physician of the early moon expedition stepped up to Rhodan.

'Eric, make sure this message is sent to Earth by hyper-wave. Dispatch it at once as follows:

'NECESSARY I REMAIN IN VEGA SYSTEM. BASE ESTAB-LISHED ON VEGA EIGHT. GOOD PROSPECTS FOR TRADE TREATIES WITH NATIVES. RETURN TO TERRA IN-

DEFINITE. DO NOT REPLY. LOCATION OF TERRA MUST
REMAIN ABSOLUTE SECRET.

STARDUST IL.

'Did you get that, Manoli?'

'Got it. Right away.'

Perry's gaze encompassed those around him. 'Friends,
thanks again for your continued loyalty. We'll meet again
soon. The Thort is preparing a big victory celebration to
which we have all been invited. And then . . .'

'The lizards!' Bell could no longer contain himself.
'What about the lizards? What's going to happen with
them?'

'Cool it, you hothead!' Perry threw a reprimand at Bell.
'I was just coming to that. And then, after the victory celebration, we'll take care of the Topides. Perhaps we'll be able
to come to an amicable arrangement with them. Chrekt-Orn
seems to be a sensible man.'

'Man!' Bell snorted in disgust. 'How can you call that
lizard a man?'

'You must learn to think in galactic terms, Reg,' Rhodan
chided. His voice grew very serious. 'What does it matter
what an intelligent life form looks like if we want to remove
the barriers between us? I don't doubt but what you're not
exactly a beauty in the eyes of the Topides, Reg. . . .'

'Nor even in our eyes,' a female voice chimed in loud and
clear from the rear of the room: Anne Sloane.

Bell spun around and cried in her direction: 'Is that how
you repay my kindness? Didn't I help you when you needed
me? I held you and let you rest your head in my lap. You
were as helpless then as . . .' Suddenly embarrassed, he
stopped, then added: 'Down below . . . in the Red Palace
. . . when we got the box from the secret time vault – what
were you all thinking then?'

He looked about but nobody answered. Only John Marshall, the telepath, grinned broadly. He was a gentleman; he wasn't telling.

A red-faced Bell stomped out of the room, leaving his friends behind. They chuckled with amusement: a man's innermost thoughts could no longer remain secret.

Not if mutants were around.

The Radiant Dome

CHALLENGE FROM THE STARS ...

Perry Rhodan had returned from the moon in Spaceship Stardust accompanied by two of the Arkonides. But the earth was on the verge of an atomic conflict. So Perry Rhodan, Peacelord of the Universe, threw an impregnable forcefield around the Stardust and declared his ship independent of the warring nations.

As he had hoped, the holocaust was temporarily averted by the more deadly threat of his allies from the stars; but could Perry Rhodan keep the peace long enough to persuade the Arkonides that mankind was fit to enter their galactic community?

THE RADIANT DOME is the second novel in the world's bestselling S.F. series. Don't miss Perry Rhodan's first cosmic adventure, ENTERPRISE STARDUST.

Enterprise Stardust

PERILOUS DAWN ...

Major Perry Rhodan, commander of the spaceship
STARDUST, found more than anyone had expected
might exist on the moon — for he became the first
man to make contact with another sentient race!

The Arkonides had come from a distant star, and
they possessed a knowledge of science and
philosophy that dwarfed mankind's knowledge.

But these enormously powerful alien beings
refused to cooperate with the people of Earth ...
unless Perry Rhodan could pass the most difficult
test any human being had ever faced ...

ENTERPRISE STARDUST is the first novel
in the Perry Rhodan series which sold
more than 70 million copies in
Europe and America.

The Lost Continent of Mu

James Churchward

MU: the Empire of the Sun, a lost culture which dominated the world 25,000 years ago. A vanished continent which sent Colonel James Churchward on a lifetime's search, from the vaults of an Indian temple to Australia, from Siberia to the South Seas.

For in 1868, while serving with the British Army in India, Churchward became close friends with a high priest who taught him how to decipher some stone tablets, hidden for centuries in the temple vaults. They told of a civilization which had emerged, flourished and decayed long before our own: the continent of Mu.

This is Churchward's story of how he followed the trail of Mu literally to the ends of the earth and of how he eventually pieced together a picture of a civilization lost in the mists of time.

PROTECTOR
LARRY NIVEN

Phssthpok the Pak had been travelling for most of his 32,000 years – his mission, to save, develop and protect the group of Pak breeders sent out into space some 2½ million years before ...

Brennan was a Belter, the product of a fiercely independent, somewhat anarchic society living in, on, and around an outer asteroid belt. The Belters were rebels one and all, and Brennan was a smuggler. The Belt worlds had been tracking the Pak ship for days – Brennan figured to meet that ship first ...

He was never seen again – at least not in the form of homo sapiens.

Larry Niven is the author of **Ringworld** which won both the Hugo and Nebula awards for the best s.f. novel of the year.